The Garden Gnomes Secret

I0636476

Dorothy M Mitchell

chipmunkapublishing
the mental health publisher

Published by
Chipmunkapublishing
PO Box 6872
Brentwood
Essex CM13 1ZT
United Kingdom

http://www.chipmunkapublishing.com

Chipmunkapublishing gratefully acknowledge the support of Arts Council England.

Author Biography

Dorothy was born in a small village in Yorkshire. Just before the Second World War. She remembers they were hard times. Air raid shelters. Sky above and over nearby towns and cities seemed to be full of enemy planes dropping their bombs. She remembers seeing fires in the distance some nights.

Her dad worked as a signalman at the local railway station. He also kept chickens for the fresh eggs and an occasional Chicken dinner. He grew his own vegetables. A must, Dorothy remembers in those long gone days of doing with less. . Her mum cleaned in the nearby pub. Dorothy remembers her mum swapping ration book stamps with other mothers. It was a regular occurrence. Sometimes her mum would need extra clothing coupons; another mum wanted extra butter. So a swap took place. It was a time of make do and mend.

In 1953 at the age of 16 Dorothy moved with her parents and brother and sister to Evesham in Worcestershire.
At the age of 18 she got married to a local lad. Her first Son Andrew was born when Dorothy was 21.
Her second Son was born when she was 27.

At the age of 37 she was diagnosed with Multiple Sclerosis. She has suffered many relapses during and since that time.

At the age of 58 She was widowed. Her life then was at extremely low ebb. She remembers her boys did what they could. But by now they had families of their own.

She was invited to the local Pentecostal church. Dorothy really enjoyed that first service. She met the Man who was to become her second husband. He had been widowed a year before Dorothy, and to cut a long story short, that was 17 years ago and much has happened to fulfill her life.

During that time, Dorothy found she had a flare for writing. In the beginning, she wrote and had published many poems, Her poetry reached many countries, and she has a small publisher in America and quite a bit has been self published. Dorothy then moved on to novels and children's books,

To her joy. Dorothy was picked up by CHIPMUNKA, They have published quite a few of her Novels. The latest to go into print is her children's books entitled SECRETS OF THE GARDEN.

"I sometimes feel like pinching myself "Says Dorothy, "I have a great deal to thank CHIPMUNKA for"

Also her thanks go to here husband Ken, Her Son's Andrew & David, Ben her Grandson, who regularly get her out of computer scrapes, her friend Martin for his input and the team at CHIPMUNKA. Who Dorothy says must all have the patience of saints.

CHAPTER ONE

BILLY'S WORKSHOP

"There, that's another gnome finished. Billy Potts sat back in his chair. He reckoned that if he carried on for another few days, the job would be done.

Billy loved his garden gnomes. He treated 'um like pals, each one had his own place. In the garden, Billy was so proud of his gnome family, as he called them.

"Well" he said to his missus Jenny, "they make a smashing talking point. They enhance the flowers and the flowers enhance the gnomes."

It had been the same every summer for the past few years. Billy would pay a visit to the hardware store, where he enjoyed choosing the different colours of paint needed for the job. The old gardener just loved giving his pals a new look. He could be found most winter days in his workshop at the bottom of his garden, busily rubbing down the old paint from last year, preparing each gnome for their new clothes.

It so amused Billy and of course Jenny Potts always knew just where to find her husband. She smiled to herself and mused "It keeps him out from under my feet."

Bill worked very hard. In spring each year, he cleared and prepared the soil ready for planting bulbs and bedding plants.

During summer he and Jenny enjoyed the beautiful flowers standing pretty proud and sentinel. And as if overseer of the colourful kaleidoscope, were Billy's little chaps were resplendent in their new clothes, looking ever so posh. The sight never failed to amuse Billy.

"By the look on their faces, I could swear they appreciate their new clothes." He had said as much to a bemused Jenny on more than one occasion.

His wife had just shaken her head. Billy was a dreamer. She had always been aware of that fact. Billy felt things deep. Billy Potts was very special. His insistence that every gnome must have a new suit every winter made Jenny smile, but she had to admit that every summer, Billy's "little chaps" as he called them always looked really nice, enhancing the garden a treat.

"Come and have a cup of tea" Jenny called from the kitchen, "You must be frozen."

Billy trudged up the garden path. Snow had fallen most of the previous night. Billy stamped his feet on the mat just inside the kitchen door trying to kick the snow from his boots.

"How many have you got to paint?" she asked.

Three more and that's the lot." Billy was sitting at the old oak kitchen table, scrubbed white now due to Jenny's insistence that the table must be kept clean. She was a stickler to it for as she pointed out, the table was used for everything, meals, cleaning the brass, and baking, so her elbow grease was essential in order that cleanliness could be maintained.

Secretly Billy thought his wife a bit of a fusspot, but he loved her anyway. The strong hot tea went down a treat.

"By gum that hit the spot Lass," he said. Jenny giggled.

"You've got blue paint on the end of your nose. I thought you were supposed to be painting your little chaps?" Billy gave a sheepish grin.

Jenny smiled fondly, "Go and get some thinners on it."
Have you finished for the day?"

The old gardener nodded, "Aye Lass."

"Well go and have a bath then.   Silvia will be bringing
Archie and Joe."

Billy sighed. He loved his grandchildren, but they were a
handful. The old man was recalling the episode with the
green paint. Both boys plastered in gloss paint, as was his
workbench. Billy was also recalling with a shake of his
head and a wry smile how Jenny had tried without success
to remove the offending green gloss paint with lard soap
and water, almost rubbing the boys' heads off, but to no
avail. Billy laughed out loud remembering the look on his
daughter in-law's face when she came to collect the boys,
finding them scalped.

Jenny had to resort the scissors, almost giving the girl a
heart attack.

"Your Dad will go mad," Silvia had retorted angrily. But it
wasn't long before she saw the funny side and calmed
down.

"Boys will be boys and the hair will grow again. You can't
keep an eye on them twenty four hours a day," she'd said
to
Jenny. Silvia didn't want to say too much. She needed
her in-laws to look after the boys when she and Fred went
off on their overseas trips.

~~~~~~~~~~~~~~

All the gnomes were finished at last. Billy always kept them
in his workshop. Well, there was no point putting them out
in the garden during the winter months.   Anyway, Billy

secretly thought to himself, his little chaps may not like cold weather. But he didn't mention this to Jenny for he had a feeling that his wife didn't really understand how he felt about his gnomes. So he told Jenny that the reason for keeping his little chaps indoors was to prevent the new paint from blistering in the frost. Jenny just smiled. Billy's little chaps were real to him and she had accepted this fact a long time ago.

Archie and Joe would be staying for a few days. It was the school holidays. The boys' Mum and Dad had planned a trip to London. They always enjoyed Christmas shopping in the department stores in the big city. It was much easier without the boys. Anyway, Silvia wanted to go to the theatre to see a favourite show.

So Silvia and Frank Potts had booked into a Hotel for a couple of nights. It would be a little break for them. And besides, the boys loved staying with their Gran and Granddad.

"Can we go and make a slide?" Joe asked his Granny.

"Well, you can if you promise not to make it on the garden path. Go round the back where it's quiet and be careful, we don't want any accidents!"

"Thanks Gran." Both boys skipped off round to the back of the house, Jenny watched as her Grandchildren disappeared from view. Joe was seven and Archie almost six. They were a couple of live wires and no mistake, Joe with his impish grin, his dark hair and eyes, foretelling the handsome man he would become, and Archie fair-haired with blue eyes, stocky, cheeky and full of mischief. Both boys much loved by their doting Grandparents.

"I will be making a hot drink in a little while. I'll give you both a call." Jenny shivered and went back into the warm kitchen.

The Garden Gnomes Secret

"Shall we make a snowman first?" Archie had gathered a pile of snow already.

"No, I'm making a slide," answered Joe, his young brother trying to shake the hard-packed snow from his gloves retorted impatiently. "I want to make a snowman first."

"Oh come on," said Joe, "a slide is much better."

Archie scuffed his feet, "Why do we always have to do what you want?"

"Cos I'm the eldest." Joe knew he would get round Archie. He smiled, "You can have the first go. Oh, come on."

With that Archie gave in. "Well, I'm making a snowman later".

It was decided that the best place to make the slide was at the side of Granddad's workshop. The area was wide enough to build a really slippery one.

So the boys set to. They found a shovel big enough and they started by levelling the snow that had drifted up the side of the workshop. When they had made the area long enough, they began to smooth it out.

The boys worked very hard until a decent slide had been made. "Wow, it's very shiny," said a very excited Joe. "Come on, let's have a go." With that, both boys trudged along the side of the newly made slide. As they did so, Archie looked into the window of Granddad's workshop. The workbench where all the newly painted gnomes were placed was situated right by the window.

"Joe, quick, one of the gnomes just winked at me."

"Don't be so daft, they're not alive," replied Joe.

Archie was adamant, "But Joe he did honest." I saw him, the one nearest to the window, the one with the green hat and jacket." Joe glared at his brother, "I'm telling Gran about you."

"Come on you two, I've made hot chocolate," said Gran.

Archie, feeling a bit upset slipped and slithered towards the kitchen closely followed by Joe. Jenny, noticing the look on the face of her youngest Grandson, asked, "What's the matter?"

Joe piped up. "He reckons one of Granddad's gnomes winked at him."

Archie turned towards his Gran. "He did Gran, honest." Archie looked at Joe. "Just because the gnome didn't wink at you," Joe retorted "you're stupid."

"Now then, that's quite enough. Don't speak to your brother like that Joe. "You mustn't call anyone stupid, it's very unkind." Jenny didn't like name-calling.

Billy realised kids argued, it was the nature of things, but he would try to salve the situation. "I watched you two playing on the slide you made. I thought what a good job you'd made of it. Can I have a go later?"

Archie laughed, "You're too big Granddad."

"Me, too big? Never, Let's finish our drinks and I'll show who's too big."

Billy and the boys arrived at the slide. "Come on then Granddad, let's see you have a go."

A pale winter sun was just setting over the workshop. The newly painted gnomes seemed to shine as the last rays shone on them. As Billy walked towards the slide he wondered if the brightness shining on the faces of his little chaps caused Archie to think one of them had winked at him earlier? The shaft of light had been particularly bright today, sort of silver in colour. It struck the old gardener as rather strange, but he had dismissed the idea. It must have been something to do with the brightness of the snow.

Billy stepped tentatively onto the slippery slide. He was too old to be doing this, but he was determined to show the boys a thing or two. He set off. The slide was just like a sheet of glass and Billy's boots with their steel toe caps didn't have any give. The old man picked up speed. "Oh, my life" he yelled, as half way along the treacherous slide he lost his balance, landing with a thud onto his bum.

Jenny, hearing the laughter, came out to see what was going on and was surprised to see a very disgruntled Billy being helped to his feet by two hysterical Grandchildren.

"I hope it's the last time you try that daft trick. Slides are for children, not silly Granddads." Trying to suppress a giggle, "You'd better have a hot bath or you won't move tomorrow.
Despite a good soak, Billy Potts was very stiff the next day.

The children stayed for another couple of days. Then it was time for them to go home. Billy and Jenny said their goodbyes. "See you soon" as they waved the boys off at the gate.

"It was lovely to see them, but it will be nice to get back to normal." Billy gave Jenny a nod. "Aye, they're hard work love." Nevertheless, he always enjoyed the boys' visits.

"I'm just going to my workshop, see you later." With that Billy set off down the path. He was glad the slide that had caused him so much embarrassment had melted. Billy opened his workshop door and scratching his head, he gazed at the sight before him.

The old gardener was a neat worker. He knew that he left his workbench tidy, and his little chaps in neat rows, their paint drying off. As Billy went closer, his eyes almost popped out of his head. The gnomes nearest to the window had all moved forward. Billy had twenty little chaps altogether. But who had moved the front five? It couldn't have been the boys! The door was securely locked; he had made sure of that when he knew his Grandchildren were coming for a visit. Well, you can't be too careful, can you?

"Are you sure you kept the door locked?" You do tend to be a bit forgetful at times.

Billy shook his head, and frowned at Jenny. "I know love" But when the boys are about, I always make doubly sure that my workshop is firmly locked. I've got some dangerous stuff in there." It isn't safe for children." Billy scratched his head once more. "It's a mystery and no mistake."

Billy tried to get the incident out of his mind. He had lots to be getting on with, clearing the ground, getting rid of debris, and preparing the soil for next spring.

CHAPTER TWO

THE MYSTERY CONTINUES

What a lovely morning. It was early April. Buds on the Magnolia tree were about to burst. Jenny loved this time of year. New growth, new beginnings, and much activity in the garden.

Billy had prepared the ground well. He always did. The spring blooms were looking a treat. He liked to have a different theme every year. This season chosen colours was to be reds and pinks. Petunia, roses, hollyhock and sweet pea would make a beautiful Cottage garden.

Billy had given each gnome, new clothes in colours to match the flowers. He did so every year.

It was time to get his little chaps out of his workshop. Billy hadn't forgotten the strange goings on that had started back in the winter time, the first being Archie's insistence that one of the gnomes had winked at him, then the moving forward of five little chaps on his workbench. Billy couldn't understand what was going on then, and he was no wiser now. Something strange was happening, but what? He had no idea what!

Billy opened the workshop door. He shook his head and blinked. This is ridiculous. Not one of his gnomes was where he had left them. They had formed a semi-circle on his workbench. Each gnome was still and motionless. They weren't alive. So how could this happen? Billy was speechless.

For years he'd had his little chaps. Most were very old, passed down to him by his Father. They were made of stone and stone couldn't move by itself. This was a mystery and no mistake. He would talk to Jenny about the funny goings on.

"Oh Billy, gnomes aren't alive. You must have moved them yourself."

Billy shook his head, "But I tell you I didn't."

"Well," Jenny retorted, "you can't blame the children, they haven't been to visit us for weeks, but they will be with us next
Week" Perhaps they can throw some light on the subject"
How can they Jenny? All this has happened since the boys went home."

Ah but don't you remember Archie telling us about the gnome that winked at him?" Billy nodded, how could he forget?

The old gardener felt uneasy. Something strange was happening. He must find out what. Jenny thought it was all stuff and nonsense. Billy was a dreamer, but she had to admit it was all a bit strange.

Silvia arrived with the boys. It was the School holidays. Archie and Joe were to spend a few days with their Grandparents again. It was a treat for them, a rest for their Mum and a busy time for Billy and Jenny. But the pair had to admit that spending time with their grandchildren was mostly enjoyable if a little tiring.

"Can we help you Granddad?"

"Yes Joe," came the reply, "If you're careful." Both boys skipped up the garden.

"You see that wheelbarrow over there?" Joe nodded. "Do you think you could bring it round to me?" The grass from the first cut of the year was piled on the lawn. "Will you

14

collect all the grass? Put it in the barrow and I'll wheel it to the back of the shed." Both boys got stuck in with enthusiasm.

"I've already prepared the flower beds, so when we've done this job, my little chaps can come out."

Billy had been waiting for this moment for ages. He knew where each gnome stood. It was the same every year.

"If you promise to be very careful, you can both help. Do just as I tell you and everything will be fine." With that the three made their way to Billy's workshop.

The gnomes were still standing in a semi-circle. It had been rather cold these past few days, rather overcast, the sun hiding behind dark clouds, so Billy had been roped in to doing a few jobs around the house for Jenny. But this morning there was no sign of rain; the sun had been shining since early morning. Good 'old Billy had escaped more housework. That was women's work anyway.

"If you're very careful you can help carry my little chaps into the garden one at a time and I will place them. I know where each one goes." The boys carefully did as Granddad asked and eventually all twenty gnomes, were standing on the path.

"Wow, that was hard work," said Granddad as he put the last one down.

Archie let out a yell. "That gnome in the blue hat and coat just wiggled at me." Billy looked to where his youngest Grandson was pointing.

"He did Granddad. Honest, he did a wiggle with his fat bum like this" and Archie proceeded to demonstrate. With both arms stuck out to the side, the lad did a sort of South

Sea Island dance. Joe, in fits of laughter, said, "Where's your hula hoop?"

"Now that's enough Joe," said Grandma.

Billy, seeing the embarrassment on Archie's face thought it best to make light of the situation. But he had to admit that he believed what young Archie was saying. The sightings by the lad confirmed to him that something very strange was going on. But what? And why was it that Archie and he were the only ones who had witnessed movement in the little chaps? It was all very peculiar indeed.

"It's your fault Billy." You must have put the idea into the lad's head. If the gnomes are moving, why haven't I seen them?"

Billy shook his head. "I don't know love. I'm as fumbled as you are."

Jenny put her hands on her hips. "There you go again, coming out with words that don't make any sense. A dreamer, that's what you are Billy Potts and you're passing the daft ideas on to the lad.

CHAPTER THREE

STUFF AND NONSENSE

There was something else that didn't add up. It was something that had been puzzling Billy ever since he had seen his little chaps move. He owned five really old gnomes. They belonged to his great-grandfather, passed on down the Potts family line to him. Billy remembered the fascinating story his father told him. It seemed that these five little chaps were special as they had been hewn from solid rock, whereas the other gnomes were made out of concrete then pressed into moulds. The special gnomes were ancient, well over a century old.

The thing that bothered Billy was the fact that he could have sworn he hadn't put the five in front. He remembered placing the twenty in rows of five as was his habit, but he was convinced he hadn't put his best little chaps in the front. The question was how did they get there?

The rows were very neat; Billy preferred it that way. He didn't like working in a muddle, but by now his mind was in a right muddle! Billy thought back to his father and the absolute love he had given his gnomes. He remembered watching as his Dad caress each of the five. Had he known the secret? How could
Billy ever find out? Billy knew he must somehow find the answer. But how?

Spring turned into summer, the garden was a blaze of colour. Billy had worked so hard. He always did every year the same. Preparing the ground in late autumn and early spring ensured a kaleidoscope of colour each summer. Billy loved it. There was another strange thing. Why did the sun seem to shine particularly bright over the garden this year? Billy mentioned the same to Mr Croft

17

next door and was surprised at his answer. "Oh, I don't think the sun is any brighter than it always is."

But Billy had noticed some particularly silvery shafts of light dancing in various parts of the garden usually around evening time. The old gardener had made all sorts of excuses why this was so. The light reflecting from his new greenhouse, and the newly erected glasshouse for Mr Croft's tomatoes. The light from the kitchen window. But however many reasons he came up with as to why his garden was "so lit up" as he put it, Billy just couldn't come up with a reasonable answer. And why was it only his garden? And more to the point, why did the silvery light only appear when he was alone?

Jenny had never seen them. It was queer, and no mistake. Every time he tried to broach the subject, Jenny shook her head, "Stuff and nonsense. It's about time you stopped all your dreaming."

CHAPTER FOUR

IT CAN'T BE TRUE?

It would soon be the school holidays again. Billy was glad, as it meant the children would be coming for couple of weeks this time. Living in the city as they did, it was good for them to experience country life, and besides young Archie had seen the gnomes move! So perhaps he would be able to see the silvery light as well?

He hadn't said as much to Jenny. Best not to. Billy would wait and see if Archie said anything. Meanwhile he would busy himself in the garden, as there plenty of jobs still to do. Billy liked a tidy garden. Besides his little chaps were becoming more mobile. He couldn't say that they moved when he was watching them. He'd tried to catch them out on several occasions. But he noticed that if he turned away and pretended he wasn't looking at the gnomes, he could swear one of his little chaps either moved his head, winked or did a tiny wiggle.
Archie had seen the wiggle and Billy reckoned he knew who the wiggler was and one day he would be quick enough.

His little chaps were playing games with him. Billy knew this, but he was unable to figure out what was going on this year. Why, was it so different?

For years he'd taken care of his gnomes, washing and cleaning each one, giving each a fresh coat of paint. Every winter, without fail. He could be found working away, making sure his little chaps looked nice for the summer. But this year, oh my, something very peculiar was going on and it was disturbing Billy. He didn't like being fuddled.

It was the third week of the school holidays. Silvia was just dropping the children off,

"Can't stop Mum" we need to be at the airport in two hours" Jenny looked at her Daughter-In law the girl was always in a rush. "Off you go." The boys will be fine.

Archie and Joe gave their Mum a kiss, they would much rather spend two weeks with Gran and Granddad than go trekking in Nepal! That would be so boring. Archie and Joe had just taken their duffel Bags to their room.

"I made cottage pie for your lunch. Is it still your favourite?"

"Yes" came the resounding reply from both boys as they tucked in, Jenny smiled.

Archie looked across the table to his Granddad. Billy winked. He'd got his ally. Now they would see if the moving gnomes were real or imagined.

"Did you bring your wellies? I need you both to get into the pond. It needs cleaning out and I can't do it."

"Is it cos you're too old Granddad?" Billy answered Joe.

"Yes, lad, that's why I waited for you two. Besides, you like messing about in water, don't you?"

The three made their way to the garden pond. They would need to very gently catch the goldfish, and put them into one of the buckets they had brought before tackling the weedy, slimy pond, and it so happened that the gnome nearest the pond was the one who Archie saw do a wiggle at him back in the spring! The boy gave the gnome a sly sideways stare. But it was just standing there, hard as rock. Solid, not doing anything.

The Garden Gnomes Secret

Archie, feeling mischievous, threw a piece of slimy weed at the gnome. It landed, splosh, on his head. The wiggly Gnome shook himself and made a gruff noise.

"Granddad, quick, he did it again. The gnome with the blue coat and hat, he did a wiggle at me." Billy and Joe, being at the other side of the pond, neither saw nor heard anything.

"Oh Archie, you're not starting that again?" It was Joe. "We haven't been here five minutes and you're at it. Gnomes can't move!" Or make a noise."

Billy came round from the other side of the pond, wiping his hands down his trousers. Which one was it, lad?"

The young boy pointed to the gnome swathed in slimy weeds. Billy tried to stifle a look of amazement. The gnome in question was displaying a different expression altogether from the one earlier. He looked cross.

Well if Billy needed any proof that his little chaps were becoming life-like and there was something very strange going on, then here it was. He leaned forward and picked up the disgruntled looking gnome, and with the tail of his shirt wiped the slimy green mess from his little chap's face. As the old gardener did this, he actually witnessed the transformation take place. For the first time, in full view of Billy, the stone gnome changed the expression on his face and looking the old man full in the face, the gnome winked. The deep blue eyes that only a few months ago had come out of Billy's paint pot had actually winked.

"Well, bless my soul." Billy was flabbergasted. He stood scratching his head, "Bless my soul," he said again.

Once more his little chap was as he had been, before the slimy weed incident. Hard, lifeless stone.

The position was becoming serious, very serious indeed. Billy examined each little chap in turn. What was going on? There was something about the demeanour of his gnomes. He couldn't put a finger on it but there was something. They looked even more alive than ever. The old gardener was perplexed. The trouble was if he brought the subject up with Jenny, Billy knew what her reply would be, "Stuff and nonsense." No, he would have to keep his worries to himself.

Billy sat down on the garden bench; Archie sidled up to him. "I saw him move as well Granddad."

The old man put an arm around the boy's shoulder, "I know you did, Lad." This situation was becoming troublesome. Billy was relieved that he wasn't the only one to see movement in his gnomes but what on earth was going on? If he hadn't been a Granddad, Billy had to admit he would be a bit scared.

Billy tried to weigh up the facts. Why after all this time of owning the gnomes, about twenty-five years to his reckoning, was this the only year he had encountered such a worry? The little chaps had been rubbed down and painted every other winter! So what was the problem this year? And why was it that only he and Archie had witnessed the gnome moving? Would he ever find out?

Jenny called from the house, "Get yourselves cleaned up, lunch is nearly ready." Billy and the boys made their way to the kitchen.

"I thought you weren't going in the pond? Just look at your clothes." Billy, feeling a bit sheepish, gave his wife a grin. "I slipped in," he said. Jenny shook her head. "Don't come to me when you've got a cold, and look at the slime on your new shirt"

Billy looked at the slime, then at Archie!   They both knew just where the horrible green stuff had come from.

After a change of clothes they all sat down to one of Jenny's meat and potato pies.

"That was good love, you make the best pies in the world."

As Billy tried to soft soap Jenny with his smooth talk, she gave him one of her knowing looks.   "Daft as a brush, that's what you are Billy Potts, and you get dafter. Gnomes that move."

You'll have the boys as silly as you if this nonsense carries on.   Young Archie is already under your spell.   Now, can we stop all this talk about gnomes moving?"

Jenny just didn't understand and Joe thought his Granddad and Archie were playing games. Well, Billy reasoned, how could Jenny and Joe know the truth, they hadn't seen any movement? This upset the old man. He wasn't making it up, nor was Archie. And there was something else that even Archie didn't know.   Billy had seen strange happenings in the middle of the night! He had first noticed the silver beam in the early hours of the morning. He had gone to the bathroom, around two o'clock. As he had passed the landing window which was directly over looking the back garden, Billy was stopped in his tracks, for there, coming from high in the night sky, was a strong shaft of silver light. The glow had become brighter and brighter, concentrating mainly around his little chaps.

As Billy gazed upon the scene, the beam of light pulsated brighter and brighter on each gnome and as it had done so, each of his little chaps raised their faces to the sky, swaying and nodding in unison.

This had occurred a couple of nights ago and knowing Jenny's reaction if he had mentioned it, Billy thought he had better keep quiet. Anyway, who knows? It was nighttime. Perhaps he'd been dreaming. But he didn't think so. He wasn't even sure he would tell Archie.

It was strange though. Not one of his neighbours had seen anything. Billy felt sure that if they had, Especially Mrs Lawson would have said something. She was noted for being a nosey parker. Didn't miss a thing. But she hadn't mentioned
Billy's gnomes once. She had mentioned though, if grudgingly, she thought His garden was looking especially nice this year.

"Your garden seems different somehow," Mrs Lawson had mentioned to Jenny. "More vibrant. Has you're Billy planted different flowers this year?" she asked. Jenny didn't think he had, but she had to admit that the garden looked particularly wonderful this season.

CHAPTER FIVE

THE OLD WRITINGS

It was August 'high summer'. The children had one-week left of their holidays. They would soon be going home. The weather had been wonderful. They had been wonderful helping Billy with the garden job and Jenny with the household chores, the latter not so enjoyable, but the boys had done their best.

"How about a day at the seaside? You've both earned a treat" The boys agreed that a day by the sea would be smashing, so the next morning they piled into Billy's old Ford and set off. The time was spent between the beach and the funfair and, of course, the café and being as they were at the seaside. Jenny saw no objection to a bag of chips for lunch and didn't they taste nice, eaten from the paper.

They did a little walking around the shops. Not Billy's idea of fun, but Jenny liked to browse and it was her day out too. As the family strolled down a cobbled side street looking into shop windows, they came to a very old-fashioned looking shop. Billy stopped in his tracks. In the front of the window amongst what appeared to be a load of junk was an old gnome exactly like one of his own. This one was lifeless, sad looking, and dirty and so far removed from how his little chaps were.

Jenny and the boys had walked on ahead, and Billy caught up with them. "Why don't you take the boys back to the beach, love. I just want to take a look round the old junk shop we've just passed." Jenny, feeling weary, agreed it would be nice to remove her sandals and rest her feet. The boys had enough of the shops and were happy to accompany their Gran to the beach.

Billy walked back to the old shop, and stepped inside. He spoke to the lady behind the counter. "How much is the old gnome in the window?"

"So, you're the person I'm expecting?" Billy looked at the old lady. Whatever did she mean? Expecting me? What was she talking about? Billy hadn't really wanted to come to the seaside. He much preferred his garden, so why had he been drawn here? It wasn't just to give Jenny and the boys a day out, no, it had been his own idea to choose Polpero. It was as though some force made him choose this particular place. But why!

"I had a dream you see, well I think it was a dream. I've had the gnome for ages. Keep him in a box out the back. I never have him on show. He's such a miserable-looking beggar, who would want to buy him?" But the dream, or whatever it was told me to put the gnome in the shop window and that a certain gentleman was coming to buy him and as nobody else has shown the slightest interest in him except you. Then I'm thinking, you must be the fellow in question."

Billy had listened transfixed. "Could you tell me all about the dream?" The old lady looked quizzically at her customer. "Well I'll tell you all I can." It was all pretty strange, very peculiar. As the old lady began to tell the tale, Billy couldn't help noticing her eyes almost violet in colour, but small and sort of screwed up. To be honest, her whole demeanour was odd. She wore a long black dress, a white apron; her grey wispy hair was tied up in a bun on top of her head. And her voice was rather squeaky.

"It was as though a silver beam of light shone on the gnome and he came to life but then it could have been a dream as I told you. I've had him for years. He was in this shop when I took over the business from my Father. That was a long time ago, but right from the start. The gnome looked miserable." The old lady gave Billy a wistful smile.

The Garden Gnomes Secret

"I always thought gnomes were jolly fellows but not him. How can a stone gnome give the impression of sadness? Would you have any idea?"

Should he put the lady in the picture? Billy decided it was the right thing to do. So he proceeded to tell her all about his own little chaps. The lady seemed genuinely interested in the story and appeared to know that she was indeed part of it. All these years, she had owned the miserable gnome without being aware that he was only part of the much bigger picture.

The old lady came from behind the counter. "Will you wait there a moment, I have something to show you." With that she disappeared behind an old faded-looking curtain that was hanging over the doorway.

Billy waited, as he did so, his eyes were drawn to the shelves bursting with jars of confectionery, Humbugs Cinder toffee, and hundreds and thousands Sugar mice Sherbet dabs. Billy Potts didn't think he had seen so many old-fashioned sweets in one shop ever before. And what about the huge boxes of chocolate? Wow.

Wasn't it strange then that amongst this entire confectionery extravaganza, Billy should come across the miserable looking gnome in a pile of junk in a Polpero sweet shop window?

The old lady stepped back through the curtain. In her hand she was holding a very old tin box. "The gnome belongs in this. Be very careful, it's very old and rather rusty. It was given to me by my father. His father passed the box down to him, and there are some bits of paper, very brown and ancient looking, something to do with the gnome, but it is of little interest to me. Think of me as the messenger or caretaker." Billy thought this statement odd, but then the whole situation was odd.

The little lady handed the box to Billy; "If you want the gnome then you'd better have the box as well. For since hearing your fascinating story, it seems the unhappy little chap had found his home at last." Billy gasped; the old lady referred to the gnome as a 'little chap'. How very strange, that was the term he used for his own Gnomes.

"Mind you, there are some as think I'm just a silly old woman or that I've gone loopy. But I believe your story. I know I'm an old romantic, but I for one think that we don't know everything and Magic does happen to the young at heart." The old lady gave Billy a twinkly smile. It struck him how old-fashioned she really was. The hem of her black dress reached the floor, her silver hair in its neat bun on top of her head and most of all her deep violet-coloured eyes! Very strange.

She handed Billy the old brown papers. Billy thanked her, saying he would read them when he returned home. The gnome was placed carefully into the tin box; the papers tucked in beside him. As Billy did this, he thought he heard a sigh coming from inside the box. He looked at the old lady and she looked at him. They had both heard the sound.

Billy paid for his purchase, tucked it under his arm, thanked the strange lady, and said Goodbye, with a promise to get in touch to let her know how things turned out. As he reached the shop door, Jenny and the boys came to meet him. "I thought you'd got lost." The day at the seaside came to an end, and the family set off for home.

"Not another one Billy? How many more gnomes?" she asked.

The old gardener grinned, "Oh, he will complete the set." Billy could hardly wait to get home, he had a feeling in his bones, that the answer to the gnome question was about to be answered, he didn't know how, but he had a strange conviction within him.

Once home, Billy hurried to his workshop with his precious purchase, young Archie tagging along behind. "Can I come Granddad?" Billy nodded, and ushered the boy towards the workshop. Once there, Archie opened the door. The old gardener placed the box he had received from the old lady gently down onto his workbench.

What would the ancient papers inside reveal? With pounding heart, Billy opened the box and removed the folded manuscript, lifting the old gnome inside, at the same time. Billy gazed in awe at the transformed face of the once miserable little chap.
As he held him, the gnome appeared to be smiling; the face that had been wrinkled and sad was now beaming with happiness.

"What does it mean, Granddad?" Young Archie hadn't been witness to the grumpy gnome, but he knew his Granddad, and judging by his excitement something wonderful must have happened.

"He was so miserable when I first saw him lad, but just look at him now." Archie took hold of the Polpero Gnome. Feeling rather perplexed, "Is this what you bought at the seaside?"

Billy nodded, "I'll tell you later, lad. "That's it you hold him while I read these ancient papers.

Billy scratched his head; there was a lot of writing he couldn't understand. He recognised 'Purchased by a Mr Algernon Potts' and a date 1760 in a place called Bavaria. Then a lot of foreign writing could be German! But he couldn't be sure. Further down the paper was a list of what could be six names, one after the other. As follows:

MOLAC
EBLAM
VERDAL
ABLEG
KITRAM
LAGREN

As Billy tried to pronounce the first sound 'M O L A C', he supposed they must be names, a most peculiar thing happened. The little chap brought back from Polpero being held by Archie gave a funny little yell. The lad, being startled, let go of the gnome. It landed on the workbench with a thud. Then to the amazement of Billy and the boy, the gnome did a sort of twirl and sat down with a bump.

For a few moments the little gnome just sat. Billy was very aware now that what had been a solid stone Gnome was portraying almost human tendencies. Flesh like features and limbs, albeit stubby dwarf like limbs with only three fingers on each hand.

Young Archie who had remained speechless till now said in a hushed voice, "What is he Granddad?"

"I don't know lad," came the reply. "I'm flummoxed. I only said Molac."

Suddenly the Polpero gnome stood up and turning to face Billy, removed his faded blue cap and bowed deeply.

"Is that your name? It must be your name!" Billy stepped closer to the little chap.

"Ask him if he can speak Granddad, I love him." Billy was proper flummoxed. What on earth was going on?

"Come on you two, what's so interesting in that old shed? Your dinner's ready."

Immediately, the gnome was returned to his stone-like state, Billy gently put the gnome back in his box and he and Archie walked towards the kitchen.

CHAPTER SIX

THE GET TOGETHER

Billy and Archie sat at the dinner table with Jenny and Joe. The meal was lovely. Usually there was a scramble for Jenny's corned beef hash, but today neither Billy nor Archie felt hungry.

"You haven't been giving him sweets have you?"

Billy tried to appear normal, "Course I haven't, love. Spoil your beautiful dinner? I wouldn't."

"Mm, I know you Billy Potts. Just lately, you've been anything but your usual self. I wish I knew was going on? What with talk of moving gnomes' secret looks between you and the boy, you'll have him as daft as you."

Joe spoke up, "Yes Gran. I've heard Archie and Granddad pretending they've seen the gnomes moving."

Actually, young Joe was a bit fed up. He knew there was something going on and he just wanted to be part of it. He hadn't seen the gnomes moving but he wanted to. He didn't believe they could move. Stone gnomes were too hard. They didn't have bones and blood, they were stone. Trouble was his brother had seen something, so had his Granddad! So why couldn't he? Joe was feeling a bit left out.

Billy, hearing the older boy's tittle-tattle, realised that yes, Joe was jealous. Why hadn't he given the boy more thought? Trouble was that at each sighting of the gnomes moving, it was only himself and Archie who had witnessed the strange sight. Billy would talk to Joe. It was only fair.

"Come with me, lads." Billy excused himself from the kitchen table. He smiled at Jenny, "That was a yummy dinner, love." Jenny smiled back "Oh go on you silly old man, you get dafter." Archie and Joe followed their Granddad outside.

Billy walked towards the workshop, both boys followed. "Now Joe, I'm going to show you something."

He went to his workbench. "You see that old box?" Billy looked towards Joe; "I want you to lift the lid, very carefully mind. It's really old." Joe did as his Granddad asked. "Now can you take out what's inside. Be very gentle mind, the contents are precious."

Joe peered into the box. "It's a gnome and what looks like some papers.

"Go on, lift him out lad." Billy was curious as to how the boy would react if the gnome moved or spoke. Joe put his hand inside the box and drew out the contents, after placing them onto the workbench. The lad looked disappointed, "He's just like the others, except he only has one thumb and what does that funny writing say?"

"MOLAC EBLAM...." Joe didn't get any further the little gnome raised himself to a standing position, turned to Billy, removed his faded blue cap, and bowed.

"Whoa, Granddad you were right, you were right! The gnomes do come alive."

Joe could hardly contain himself. "Why didn't I see them move before? Why hasn't Granny seen them?" Then to the utter amazement of Billy and the boys, the gnome began to speak.

"You see me only if you believe. Billy has always known and believed. Let me tell you the story of the six gnomes and how Billy was able to reunite me with my five brothers."

"Many, many years ago, my brothers and I were hewn out of very old stone by an old Bavarian peasant. He had magic powers. He loved us all very much, and we loved him, but he was dying." A Mr Algernon Potts was travelling through Bavaria and got to know, and like the old peasant, he listened to the old man's magic and was informed that we would survive down the years but only if we were loved and this being the case, then the magic spell put on us by the old peasant meant we would be brought to life every hundred years by a special Gnome Beam through the power of love.

Mr Algernon Potts stayed with the old man, caring for his needs until the old Bavarian passed away. It was also obvious that Mr Algernon Potts loved us. We survived through the years because the six of us have been passed down the Potts family. Firstly by Mr Algernon Potts who had great love for us. He so liked the Bavarian way of life that he decided to make his home there. He helped the old man who passed on his magic powers to him.

"When the old peasant died, Mr Algernon Potts decided to make his way back to England, bringing the magic with him. He made his home in London where we all lived happily for many years. The six of us, though back in our stone like state, were able to realise that it would be many years before the Gnome Beam would come again, to bring us to life. That would only happen if the people who owned us continued to love us."

"Mr Algernon married and had a Family two little girls named Emily and Patience. They loved us very much. We so wanted to tell them we loved them too, but because of the spell we weren't able to."

Billy and the boys listened to all the gnome had to tell them in hushed silence.

"You must be very old then?" Archie spoke in a whisper, "You really are magic."

Billy asked, "How did you get separated from your brothers and when?"

The little chap gave a long drawn out sigh, "Well, it's like this. Although most of the Potts family has been kind to my brothers and me, there was one who was really horrible, an old seafaring blaggard by the name of Silas Potts. If it hadn't been for the kindness of his wife Lucinda, his long suffering wife, conditions would have been much worse for us."

Billy and the boys were intrigued. "Please do go on." The gnome gave a little cough.

"It takes some telling, but I'll try. Well, it was like this, the man in question would have been your great, great, great grandfather. The rotten apple of the family. Took to drink in his early years and went whaling but couldn't stand the slaughter. But he liked the money that the oil and blubber brought in. While he was at sea, life was peaceful for Lucinda Potts. She looked after the cottage, the tiny garden, and us. For you see Lucinda was full of love. She had been witness to the Gnome Beam and Gnome Beam night, when my brothers and I were brought to life."

"So it was time for the hundred year awakening in Lucinda Potts' time?" Billy was awe-struck, as were the boys.

"Did Silas ever see you alive?" It was Joe asking the question all three wanted the answer to.

Lagren turned to the boy. "No, he didn't, how could he? The man was a drunkard and nasty with it. No love in him, none at all.   Eventually his drunken ways were to be his downfall. On his return home, from what was to be his last whaling trip, blind drunk as usual he set about Lucinda. She tried to tell him about my brothers and I coming to life, thinking no doubt that the news may please him and make him happy. But no, in his disbelief and anger Silas Potts ran out into the garden, picked me up and threw me in the direction of Lucinda. She side-stepped, and I smashed into the wall."

"But unfortunately for Silas, the man was so drunk that as he threw me that he lost his balance, tripped over a large stone, hitting his head on the ground. Silas Potts died where he fell. Nobody missed him much. Unfortunately for me, however, I stayed where I landed, hidden behind bushes for a very long time and in the impact, I lost my right thumb."

Archie, transfixed by the story, whispered, "Oh you poor little thing. Does your hand hurt?"

"Well, I suppose it did at the time," answered Lagren "but the minute I turned to stone the pain stopped"

Billy spoke now, "Well, this is a mystery and no mistake." How did you manage to get separated from your five brothers?"

"Well, after the death of Silas Potts, Lucinda decided to move away. It was horrible for me. I had returned to stone, as had my brothers, so although I was unable to move, I was aware of everything that was going on. In her haste to get away to begin a new life, Lucinda packed her belongings and moved south, forgetting all about me! Perhaps she couldn't find me? Perhaps she thought I was broken? Anyway for whatever reason, I was left behind, trapped in my stone body. The next people who lived in the Cottage didn't have any children, but they were keen gardeners. They found me."

"They also found the old tin box that we travelled from Bavaria in which also contained the old brown papers with the names that the old peasant had given each of us and not wanting me, probably because I looked so miserable, they gave me to the old man who owned the shop next door."

Billy was dumbstruck. "So how did the gnomes get to me from Lucinda?"

Lagren smiled, "Love must be the answer, but I admit there is a mystery to this story. Perhaps together we will find the truth.

Billy and the boys listened absolutely enthralled to everything the little gnome had told them. Joe, wide-eyed and incredulous, turned to his Granddad.

"I didn't believe in magic at all, but oh boy, I do now." Billy addressed the gnome; "I think its time to reunite you with your five brothers. How do I introduce you?"

"Call me Lagren. My brothers will know me."

Meanwhile, the five stone gnomes and the other, lesser concrete ones had been aware that something important must have been happening. Billy and the boys had been in the workshop for ages. The five especially could sense something big was about to happen.

Billy carried LAGREN and the old box containing the papers along the side of his workshop. The boys followed. "Ready then?"

Lagren nodded.

Billy and the boys walked into the garden, and over to where the group of gnomes was standing absolutely still.

What happened next was so unexpected that even Billy couldn't have foreseen the reaction of his five little chaps. When they were introduced to their long lost brother, LAGREN the Polpero gnome seemed to stand erect. Gone forever, was the miserable demeanour he had displayed when Billy had found him the quaint old shop. He was regal and proud.

His five brothers hadn't uttered a word. The shock of seeing Lagren again after all these years had surprised them all. Then, as if by magic, MOLAC Full of life, tears of joy in his eye, stepped forward.

"My long lost brother after all these years, I never thought to see you again." As he spoke, the rest of the brothers started to move forward in unison towards Lagren and Molac. What happened next brought tears to Billy's eyes. From somewhere close by sweet voices accompanied by gentle music could be heard, and as if by magic, the six brothers began to sway in time to the melody.

Archie and Joe, who were witnessing this strange scene, stood mesmerised. "What are they doing Granddad?"

Billy, awe-struck, said "I don't know lad, it must be a ritual dance of happiness, and love." As they watched, the lesser gnomes began to sway with stiff robotic movement.

After a while, Lagren raised his hands and the music stopped. "We must talk my brothers. I will tell you of my sometimes terrible adventures and you must tell me how you have faired down the years."

Billy and the boys listened, transfixed, while the brothers told the most unbelievable, awesome, stories, they had ever heard or been part of. Stories of the hundred year awakenings, strange lights, secret signs, funny creatures, and the need for secrecy and love to ensure the gnomes continued to survive down the years.

Billy was eager to see what would happen now, for he was sure that much more magic would unfold. And the old man could hardly wait.

CHAPTER SEVEN

GNOME BEAM NIGHT and JENNY'S DREAM

The children would soon be returning home it was almost time for them to go back to school, and frankly, after such a wonderful holiday with Gran and Granddad and the gnomes (nobody would believe them about the gnomes). So Archie and Joe made a pact that the business of the gnomes would remain a secret even from their Mum and Dad. The secret must remain just that, a secret the boys would be able to keep quiet after listening to everything that Lagren and the other gnomes had shared with them. Granddad had said it was a great privilege to be trusted with such news. And it was, the secret was locked away in their hearts forever. Archie and Joe didn't know it yet, but they were in for the time of their lives.

Billy and the boys didn't have long to wait, for unbeknownst to them, magical forces had been at work. The Gnome Beam, which was now at its maximum power, was getting ready to do the job it had done all down the years. This was to bring all the Potts gnomes into full life and in so doing, ensuring that the spell of love put on them by the old Bavarian Peasant came to fruition every hundred years, providing love accompanied them.

Well, it would appear the conditions for this year's awakening had passed the test. The last Saturday in August had been Gnome Beam night since the old Peasant in Bavaria had made the six gnomes, giving them special, magic powers. He had created the Gnome Beam and deemed that for as long as love survived between the Potts family the Beam of Light would continue to shine its special brilliance onto the gnomes every hundred years.

This had been the gift to Algernon Potts for his kindness to the Peasant. A strange gift you may say, but the old

The Garden Gnomes Secret

Bavarian wanted to make sure his gnomes went on forever. He saw in Algernon Potts a truly gentle and loving man. He prayed that this trait would continue down the years. He knew he had to die shortly but his gnomes would live forever.

"It was almost the end of August," Lagren spoke now, "It is time my brothers. We must prepare for Gnome Beam night." So one by one Molac, Eblam, Ableg, Verdab and Kitram stepped forward. "Do you all remember what we must do" The brothers nodded.

While the lesser gnomes waited and looked on, the six brothers formed a semi-circle, It was early evening, the weather was warm and balmy not a cloud in the sky. It appeared that the garden was changed. A soft light bathed the flowers, bringing out subtle shades that weren't normally seen. From somewhere above, gentle music could be heard.

The brothers in unison as if remembering without being told what was required of them, raised their arms to the sky.

From far in the distance a pinpoint of light appeared. It could have been a star, but the star got bigger and bigger and brighter and brighter. As the brothers swayed, their arms reaching up to the sky, the light formed into a circle surrounding the six gnomes. So brilliant was it that Billy and the boys had to shield their eyes.

By this time, Archie and Joe were to say the least absolutely awe struck. Was all this real? And if it was, why was it happening to them? They felt part of something wonderful. They thought of what they had been witness to so far, it must be

Magic? It made the youngest brother shiver and he felt a bit scared, but it was a funny scared. Granddad, Joe and he were part it. Granddad wasn't frightened so why should he be?

The Beam of Light came closer and closer and as it did so became softer, not as brilliant to the eye. Soft dreamy music continued to play, it seemed to encapsulate the whole of Billy's garden. While everything beyond was ordinary and unchanged.

Joe pointed his finger skyward and spoke in a hushed whisper "Look Granddad."

From the centre of the Beam of Light, gliding downwards almost like bubbles, each one a different colour, where these balls of light. When they came closer, Billy and the boys were able to make out about a dozen.

"Look, they're all smiling Granddad, and they have four arms." Billy estimated that each orb would be as big as a beach ball. They had lovely smiling faces, with four arms on each creature and hands with six fingers on each. Each ball carried a shiny gold-coloured tray.

Time had moved on a pace. It was now early evening. "Good grief, Jenny will be wondering what on earth is going on." Billy excused himself, and went looking for his wife. He found her fast asleep in her favourite chair. This surprised Billy, for Jenny wasn't the sort who liked a nap in the daytime. Billy touched sleeping beauty gently on her shoulder.

"Alright love?" he asked her. Jenny awoke with a start.

"What on earth am I doing?"   How long have I been asleep?"

Don't know love, I just came in from the garden." Are you feeling alright?"

Jenny gave Billy a questioning look. "I can't really say for sure."

Billy a little concerned, "Perhaps you'd better go to bed, and I'll bring you a milk drink."

Jenny, felling anything but herself, decided to take Bill's advice. Why did she feel so sleepy?

Billy returned to his garden. He stood in amazement. There had been yet more changes. The six brothers were fully mobile. The lesser gnomes were sat in-groups sort of moving robotically. Joe and Archie were so engrossed with the brothers that they didn't see Billy come back into the garden.

Molac was talking to the boys. "Yes, the spheres of coloured light that come down the Gnome Beam are called Beamins. They have always attended Gnome Beam night." They are part of the magic spell that was given to the Potts family by the old peasant in Bavaria all those years ago."

"Well, what do they do?" Archie asked.

Molac turned to face the boy. "It will soon be party time, known as Gnome beam night. Ask yourself where the refreshments are if it's to be a party."

Archie and Joe looked around; "There isn't any food."

"Well," said Molac, "Do you see the trays that the Beamins are carrying?" Archie, wide eyes, nodded.

With that Molac raised his hand. In a flash, one of the Beamins was hovering in front of the gnome. "Now Archie, what is your most favourite meal?"

The boy dragged his eyes from the hovering Beamin. And looking at Molac in disbelief, "Egg and chips, with tomato sauce."

"Okay, Archie, if you ask the Beamin, your meal will appear on the tray he is carrying."

Joe said, "My best meal is Mum's Roast dinner." In a flash, one after the other, the meals appeared. It was magic. Molac bade the two dumbfounded boys to be seated at the garden table. The piping hot dinners looked so appetising that the boys could hardly wait to tuck in.

The smiling Beamin said in a tinkly voice, "Please enjoy." Then he hovered for a while in front of Molac. It seemed they were having a conversation when, to the amusement of both boys, the Beamin floated up to Billy's Magnolia tree and sat on one of the branches.

Archie in an excited voice asked his Granddad what he thought the Beamins were doing there? All of a sudden it became clear, for the Beamins started to glow, each one in his own colour. A kaleidoscope of lights shone like baubles on a Christmas tree.

It was about 9:30 in the evening and Jenny was still sleeping. Billy checked her every now and again, but each time he found her fast asleep. There were some mighty strange things going on lately and they all centred round the gnomes.

The night was warm and everyone in the garden was happy. The six brothers were especially joyful; being united after all these years apart was a miracle.

Billy and the boys were having the best time ever. The old gardener wished Jenny could be in the garden to enjoy the most beautiful evening. But unbeknownst to him, magic powers were taking place to make his wish come true.

Billy had decided to build a bonfire. If he was very careful and didn't make the fire too big, then the bottom of the garden would be ideal. It was away from the house and flowers. There was plenty of wood by the side of the shed. This would be fine to start the fire going. He had lots of garden waste to burn.

As he busied himself collecting wood and stacking it safely into piles, a familiar figure walked slowly towards him. Billy, startled, dropped the pile of wood he was carrying. He rubbed his hands down the side of his trousers and scratching his head spoke to the visitor

"You're the old lady from the shop in Polpero. "How on earth did you get here?"

The strange lady smiled, "'Twas the Gnome Beam that brought me."

Billy was flummoxed, "But I don't understand."

The old lady smiled. "I have been a part of this story for a very long time. Let me explain. My family line goes right back to the peasant in Bavaria, but unfortunately, my ancestors had no real love for the gnomes. They didn't even like them and as the old Bavarian informed your ancient relatives, it is love that enabled the gnomes to continue down the years. But allow me to tell you of the spark of love that enabled me to be involved. It was ordained by a stronger force than you or me that we should meet."

"It was as though the magic lay dormant for a time, probably something to do with the evil portrayed by Silas Potts, upsetting the path of love, down the Potts line. Fortunately, snippets of love came down my family tree, just enough to enable us to meet and you to find Lagren, allowing the sad lost gnome to be reunited with his brothers."

Billy interrupted, "But I thought you didn't like the gnome?"

The old lady paused, "It seemed a long time waiting for the next Gnome Beam night, knowing I couldn't do anything until we met. It was rather frustrating for me. The old lady felt around in her pocket and pulled out a tiny parcel. She looked at Billy, "I feel sure you will know what to do with this?"

Billy took hold of the tiny green velvet cloth tied with ribbon and opening the parcel, he gasped in amazement! In his hand was a tiny stone thumb! "Good gracious, I never expected this." Billy thanked the old lady. After beckoning a Beamin to give his visitor anything she required, Billy excused himself. He must go and see Jenny.

After reaching the bedroom, he was surprised to find his wife dressed in her finest party dress. "Oh sweetheart, I like the Frock." Billy couldn't remember Jenny looking more beautiful.

"Something woke me, a bright light and I feel wonderful." Billy was happy for his wife but he had to admit she didn't seem her usual self. It was as though Jenny was in a dream.

She made her way downstairs. "Oh Billy, listen to that beautiful music." As they reached the kitchen door, Joe and Archie met them. "Come on Granny, this is a smashing party. Where have you been?" inquired a very excited Archie.

Jenny, in a daze, looked around her. This was their garden, but it wasn't. Why was everything so bright and cheerful, what on earth were those coloured lights floating round the garden and where was that beautiful music coming from? This must be a dream.

The Garden Gnomes Secret

"What would you fancy to eat Gran?" Jenny looked towards her youngest Grandson. "What do you mean? I haven't prepared anything Archie." The boy chuckled, "You can ask for anything you like and a Beamin will bring it on a shiny tray."

Granddad piped up, "Just enjoy the party love. I'll explain later."

Jenny shrugged her shoulders, "If you can't beat 'um, join 'um." She was enthralled at what was going on and seemed to become strangely accepting of the whole affair.

"I bet they can't bring me my favourite meal?"

"What's that then Granddad?"

Billy smiled at Joe. "Okay lad, go and ask a Beamin to bring me a lovely big steak and a plate of chips. I won't be a moment. I must go round the back and make sure the bonfire is safe." And at the same time he would be able to check that the old lady had asked for her favourite meal.

After searching the area thoroughly, Billy could find no sign of her. He felt in his trouser pocket. Yes, the tiny parcel was still there! So she must have been in the garden and there was the tiny tray containing a few crumbs left over from whatever the old lady had eaten.

The whole situation was becoming stranger by the minute. No one else had been in that part of the garden, so nobody other than himself had seen the old lady! Come to think of it, she was dressed in exactly the same clothes she had been wearing when he first met her in the quaint shop in Polpero! Odd, very odd.

Jenny seemed enthralled and strangely accepting of the whole affair. Not at all normal behaviour for her. A no-nonsense sort of woman usually.

"Come on Granny, tell the Beamin what you would like to eat." Archie was almost beside himself with excitement. What an adventure the boys were having, a real life magic story and it was all taking place in their Granddad's garden. Wow!

"Well, my absolute favourite is a nice egg salad followed by a banana split."

No sooner had the words left Jenny's mouth than a beautiful egg salad, with all the trimmings, plus a scrumptious-looking banana split, appeared on a tray carried by a shiny pink Beamin.

Billy arrived back to find Jenny tucking in. No sooner had he sat down beside his wife than another Beamin, bright purple in colour, brought a tray of steak and chips. The old man rubbed his hands together, and began to tuck in to the gorgeous looking feast of succulent steak and chips. Billy gazed round his garden, now completely transformed from the one he had always known.

All the Beamins were sitting in the old Magnolia tree, taking it in turns to serve the family with whatever meal they desired. Heavenly music played from somewhere high in the summer sky. After everyone had eaten their fill, Billy suggested they sit around the fire and tell stories and sing happy songs.

The six brothers clapped and cheered as they made their way to the fire. Following on behind came the lesser gnomes, stiff and robotic in movement. They inched forward, making grinding, scratching noises as they moved.

"Look at the gnomes Granddad, don't they seem happy?" Billy nodded to his youngest grandson. What an adventure they were having. Wasn't it fortunate for the boys that the hundred-year awakening was taking place right now and they were here to witness the extravaganza. Billy shook his head; he was finding it hard to come to terms with any of this.

The festivities carried on in this vein well into the night, with Beamins flying here and there at intervals, the beautiful rainbow colours of each creature flashing as they intermingled with each other. The fire burned brightly, crackling and spitting out sparks of red, gold and amber, as if competing with the colourful Beamins for Prominence.

Joe meantime was in his element. The lesser gnomes held a fascination for the boy. He was intrigued to know just how they worked and where was the mechanism that enabled each one to move? Joe picked up one gnome, then another, giving each one a shake as he did so, trying to find a button or a some device to turn them on, when all of a sudden Joe heard a disgruntled groan coming from the lesser gnome he holding.

Molac took charge, "No boy, please don't do that, the lesser gnomes aren't toys. Neither are my brothers or myself. We are all real gnomes." Admittedly, the lesser gnomes are as yet only able to move in a primitive way, but if the love that enabled my brothers to continues down the years carries on and if that love is uppermost in the hearts of the Potts family, then we will survive, and be brought back to life every hundred years, with the lesser gnomes growing more and more agile and at each party time growing more like my brothers and me. It may take hundreds of years. Who knows, if love for us gnomes carries on as it has then eventually the lesser gnomes will be able to move and talk like myself, and my brother. Mind you, I Molac will always be leader number two."

"Is that the time?" Jenny was looking at her watch, "1:30 in the morning? The boys should be in bed, Billy. Silvia would go mad if she knew they were up this late."

Billy gave one of his pearls of wisdom answers, "What Silva doesn't know isn't going to hurt her. As it's such an unusual party and they are having a wonderful time, it won't hurt for once, love."

Jenny accepted without argument. Billy was quite right; it was indeed a lovely party, and the best she had ever enjoyed. Jenny smiled and nodded her approval.

Billy replenished the fire with more wood and after making sure it was safe, he sat back on one of the garden chairs going over in his mind all that had happened this year right back to last winter when he had given his little chaps their new clothes. Then on to spring, when he and Archie had seen the first wink and wiggle. It was then that Billy began to realise that this year was like no other. Would life for the Potts family ever be the same again? For what Billy hadn't realised was that the Peasant magic was a special kind of magic. Billy would find out at a later date.

The old man felt the thumb in his pocket. He must find Lagren. Billy found the gnome in conversation with Archie. The young lad was sitting cross-legged, elbow on knee, fascination on his face as Lagren told him of his life with his brothers.

"Yes, we came all the way from Bavaria many, many years ago. We were all together until that fateful day Lucinda Potts left me behind when she moved south. She must have thought me broken and I can't blame her."

Archie looked at Lagren. "Why, what happened?"

Lagren took a deep breath, "Well, it's like this, Lucinda's husband was a drunkard. He treated his wife pretty bad." Lagren continued to tell the boy the story of the hundred year awakening in Lucinda's time, how in a fit of drunken rage and Silas Potts had thrown him at Lucinda, which the lady had side stepped. A cloud of the unhappy memory showed in the eyes of the gnome. "I hit the garden wall with such force that Lucinda must have thought me damaged beyond repair. I lay in agony for quite a long time."

Sadness came into the eyes of the child. "Oh yes, gnomes can feel pain, be it physical or the heartbreaking pain of separation. The Bavarian peasant made sure of that, for how can we feel love, if we cannot also feel pain?"

As Billy listened to the story Lagren was telling, he thought how privileged the Potts family was to be part of such a fascinating gnomic and Potts' history. A magic history that surely set them apart. No one else had such a fascinating story to tell. A story that had been played out over many years. Who would believe it though?

Billy listened to everything Lagren had to say overawed by the revelations, he thanked the gnome and took his leave to find Jenny. The five brothers surrounded his wife. They were singing in perfect harmony to the music coming down the Gnome Beam. Billy listened in wonder. Why, it must be coming from Heaven. Molac was singing in beautiful baritone, Eblam, Verdag, Kitram and Ableg harmonised beautifully, although Billy couldn't help noticing that one little chap was rather flat. He thought it was Kitram, but no matter.

Jenny appeared to be enjoying the serenade. The Beamins hummed along from the branches of the Magnolia tree. Joe and Archie did their best to join in. Who would believe they had been singing with gnomes? They weren't about to tell anyone, certainly not their friends at school. Nobody must know.

Billy waited until the singing had finished. He thought it far too beautiful to disturb. But now Billy was about to make the day even better for one little chap. The old man called Lagren to one side and from his trouser pocket he took out the green velvet parcel and handed it to the puzzled gnome. Lagren opened it.

"My thumb! My thumb! How? When?" Lagren held the surprise in his hand and without another word, the little gnome did something that was to stay with Billy for the rest of his life. As the old man stood hands on hips smiling down at the gnome, Lagren put both arms around the leg nearest to him and began to weep. Not tears of sadness, but tears of joy.

Billy, taken aback by this show of affection, stooped and lifted the little gnome into his arms. The gardener proceeded to explain that the old lady from the shop in Polpero had come across the thumb and had brought it back to the party earlier this evening. "It seems your thumb was never really lost, just mislaid."

All the other gnomes, hearing the commotion, came over to Billy and Lagren. There was much cheering when the gnomes heard the good news, about their brother's happy news. And it wasn't long before Billy was able to put the thumb back where it
belonged. It took special magic glue to do the job.

The boys asked about the thumb. Billy just smiled, "It's all part of the magic lads, the lovely Magic."

Lagren was seen beaming from ear to ear for quite a long time.

At 3:30 in the morning, Jenny decided she would go back to bed. She felt tired, but it was a different sort of tired. Her spirit felt uplifted and she was happy and relaxed. What had been going on? This wasn't real; perhaps she was in a dream? A lovely, magical dream.

The Beamins, seeing Jenny making a move, gathered round her as she made her way to the stairs. The coloured orbs began to hum a lullaby whilst they escorted the happy Jenny to her room.

CHAPTER EIGHT

BACK TO NORMAL, OR IS IT?

By now it was almost dawn. Birds were awakening from their slumber. Billy was very tired and a funny thing, Joe and Archie had fallen fast asleep on the lawn. He had carried them both to bed earlier in the evening, waiting by their beds until they were both fast asleep. Billy was aware of something else. His little chaps were all making their way slowly to their very own spot in the garden where they stood ever since Billy had owned them. As the old man watched, the Gnome Beam seemed to envelop each gnome.

The Beamins took their place in the centre of the Beam and as Billy watched in wonder, the Beam made its way skyward before disappearing into the speck of light from whence it came. The old man looked around his garden and as the first rays of
late Autumn sun shone down on the scene, Billy saw, with a feeling of sadness, that all in his garden was as it had been, not only since the party, but long before, when he and Archie had witnessed the first wiggle and wink.

As Billy gazed around his neat garden, he noticed with a tear in his eye that his little chaps were all as they had been, all the years he had owned them. Each one was standing in the place he had chosen for them. The six stone brothers in places of prominence while the lesser gnomes stood where Billy had placed them, where they best enhanced to flowers, and the flower's showed the gnomes off.

The old man blew his nose loudly and wiped his eyes, and walked over to where the six gnomes were standing. Billy looked at Molac who, like all the rest, was just standing inanimate, lifeless cold stone.

Billy felt his heart his heart was going to break, but why? The old gardener couldn't understand any of this. If what Lagren and Molac had told him was true and the magic only happened every hundred years, then neither he nor the boys would ever see the little chaps come to life ever again, he couldn't bear it.

The months passed and they do say time is the healer. The boys had gone home after what to them had been the best holiday at Granny and Granddad's ever. But there was another mystery after Gnome Beam night. The boys said very little about the party, so Billy reckoned that what they had been told and witnessed at that magical party, about the boys keeping the secret, and that it would remain locked in their hearts forever, must be true. Silvia and Frank had never made any mention of
gnomes 'coming to life' so the boys must have kept their word or the secrecy magic had worked.

As autumn turned into winter, Billy was once again in his workshop preparing the paint and brushes for the job he had done every year. But this year he knew it was going to be different! How could it not be so? His little chaps who for one very special Gnome Beam night had come into full life were now, as they had been ever since Billy had owned them, Stone gnomes. But it had been real. That special night, it wasn't a dream? The old gardener felt a warm glow inside, honoured to be part of the adventure.

Winter was making its presence felt, the north wind howled around the workshop. Billy was snug as a bug. Last night's snowfall lay thick on the ground. He had almost completed rubbing down and painting the lesser gnomes. They did look nice. The old man needed to make an extra special job for all his little chaps from now on, after all he knew the secret and he would do his part in this unusual venture to make sure the legend continued down the years and the gnomes would live on. For who knows? The next Gnome Beam night in a hundred years time could see the lesser gnomes being more like his six special chaps? But that was a long way ahead, to be enjoyed by another generation of the Potts family. Perhaps another Billy Potts!

Billy had to admit that he kept the best 'til last. He always enjoyed giving the five stone gnomes their new clothes, now it was six. To Billy they had always seemed more life-like, even before Gnome night and the Gnome Beam. The old man picked up Molac. As he gently caressed his pal, Billy noticed that the little gnome had one eye closed. The old man could have sworn that Molac had both eyes open when he brought him in from the garden earlier. As Billy pondered the situation, the closed eye slowly opened.

Just for a moment, Billy experienced a tender moment. It was as though Molac was trying to convey a sign to his old pal, telling him that everything was as it should be and all would be fine.

In the next instant the Billy noticed a feeling of peace within his heart. It had been a sign to him, he knew his little chap had wanted to reassure him. He placed the now inanimate gnome back on the workbench.

Jenny was also experiencing something odd. While trudging in the snow to take Billy a hot drink, she had come across a tiny green velvet pouch. "What do you think this is?" Billy sipping his cocoa shook his head, but of course, the old boy knew full well what the velvet pouch was and the precious cargo it had carried.

But Billy made light of the question, "Perhaps it held some precious treasure love."
The old man, not wanting to tell a lie, thought that was the best way out of the situation. Billy held out his hand, Jenny gave the green velvet pouch to her hubby. Billy placed it gently in his pocket.

The Garden Gnomes Secret

When this year's paint job had been done, and all Billy's little chaps were looking brand spanking new, he sat back. What an extraordinary year this had been, right back to last spring when the first wink and wiggle had happened, then on to the slime in the pond fiasco. Billy recalled the telling off from Jenny!

As for wonderful Gnome Beam night, Billy Potts knew that for the remaining years of his life he would never forget the magic of this special time. He realised many things about the whole he would never really understand, but then did he need to? He had been part of a magical event that was so special, as had the rest of the family. But Billy felt that he was the only one who would remember in full everything that had happened. The boys and Jenny would only remember in part.

So how was he going to ensure that the magic continued down the Potts family line?

CHAPTER NINE

POLPERO and THE PROMISES

Winter turned into spring, bulbs were once again bursting from the ground. Billy loved this time of year, new growth, and new start. The boys were expected once again.

Silvia and Frank were off to some outlandish place, hitch-hiking around Mongolia.

"Must have more money than sense," Jenny had mused, but she didn't mind having the boys for a couple of weeks in the school holidays and the lads loved it so.

Their help in the garden would be extra welcome this year; the chest infection their Granddad had suffered in the winter was gone now. But Jenny felt he needed to build up his strength, "Stuck out in that workshop in all weathers," she'd said to the stubborn old man, but it was water off a duck's back.

Archie and Joe arrived full of beans and raring to go. They got stuck into the garden work. "When can we bring the gnomes out, Granddad?" Billy glanced at the boy. Archie walked over to Billy's side. "I do remember Granddad. It's our secret, the Potts' family secret and my name is Potts." I love them, and if we keep the love going down the years there will be a Gnome Beam night in another hundred years.

Billy gave Archie a hug, "I know you do lad." The old gardener was touched by what his grandson had said. There was a special quality in the lad, gentleness. Joe was similar. They were both blessed with the magic quality needed for this assignment. Billy just felt in his heart that Archie had that special something he couldn't put his finger on.

The Garden Gnomes Secret

Jenny decided that a day at the seaside would do them all good, the bracing sea air was just what Billy required to put the roses back in his cheeks, the boys excited at the prospect helped to fill the old car with everything required for a day by the sea.

They reached Polpero mid-morning, the sun was shining. Seagulls made their plaintive cries. The place wasn't too crowded. The family found a favourite spot on the beach, and the boys began to make the usual fort-like castle with moat and
drawbridge, this latter ingenious contraption made from platted lollypop sticks faithfully collected and saved.

Jenny sat in her deckchair and began to knit the socks she had been making for ages. Knitting was her hobby. Mind you, Billy didn't like the knitted socks she made for him, they rubbed his corns. But not wanting to hurt his wife's feelings, Billy wore them out as soon as possible.

"I'm just going for a stroll love." To be honest, sitting on the beach was boring for the old man. Jenny looked up from her knitting, "Okay, see you later, the boys are fine."

Billy made his way into the streets of the quaint old town. He was eager to pay a visit to the little lady and the old-world shop. As he walked along the cobbled streets, however, he was unable to find what he was looking for. Up and down, up and down, but he was unable to find the old lady's shop.

"Can you help me to find the little shop and the old lady?" he asked people who were behind counters in their own shops, only to be told the same thing over and over, that nobody knew the shop, nor the old lady!

Billy hurried back to the beach. "Jenny, do you remember the old lady in the quaint shop I told you about?" You know, where I found Lagren?" You remember?" he was in the front of the window?" Jenny shook her head, "Oh Billy, it could have been any shop window, they were all oldie-worldly looking, and I certainly don't recall any old lady." Sorry love, I can't help you.

Billy realised that he had been the only person to see the little old lady. Yes, of course, it must be all part of the magic. She had been sent to enable Lagren to be reunited with his brothers. So she and he were the means of getting the little gnome back where he belonged. Some force overseeing the whole situation, knowing of Billy's great love and lifelong commitment to his 'little chaps' must have created the situation for this to be achieved. The great force for love knew Billy Potts would generate enough 'Gnome love' ensuring that it would continue down the Potts Family line. And if Archie and Joe Potts were anything to go by then everything pointed to the next hundred-year awakening being as resounding a success as the one they just enjoyed.

The family returned home after their day trip. Billy was disappointed that he hadn't found the Polpero shop or the little old lady, but he knew it was magic and it had been there last time they came. He decided to say no more on the subject to Jenny. She didn't understand fully what had occurred. To her, it was all stuff and nonsense.

The garden was at its best. Summer sun shone on flowers and gnomes alike, each plying for prominence, each portraying their own kind of beauty. Billy was sitting in his old garden chair enjoying the peace. He loved his garden. He loved his little
chaps. This to him was the best place on earth. Contented, the old man drifted off to sleep.

Jenny found Billy early in the evening. The old gardener had passed away, Molac cradled in his arms.

On the day of the funeral, young Archie stood by the side of the coffin. "I will always love your little chaps, Granddad, and I will always love you. So will Joe. We will do our best to make sure the love goes on and on and they make the next Gnome Beam night in a hundred year's time."

Among the floral tributes was a tiny posy from 'KITRAM, EBLAN, ABLEG, VERDAG, MOLAC and LAGREN

~ THE END ~

Further Secrets of the Garden

Dorothy M Mitchell

PREFACE

Jenny had found her husband Billy in his garden chair. He had passed away with a smile on his face, and in his arm he was holding his favourite gnome. The one called MOLAC. The old gardener had died a happy man. He knew all about the secret. What he hadn't bean aware of though was the adventures Archie and Joe were going to be involved in, because of their love for the Gnomes. This was a pity. Billy Potts would have enjoyed the adventure.

Dorothy M Mitchell

.

CHAPTER 1

THE MOVE

Billy's parents lived to a good age, and passed away within months of each other. One of John Potts last words to his son were; "Take care of the gnomes and love them, Remember my words Billy remember them well and you will be witness to such magic powers, powers that will astound you"
Billy Pots had been amazed by what he had been a part of, his dad had been right; Billy and his own grand children had witnessed such breathtaking magic, Magic so incredible and beautiful. Billy Potts had died a happy man.

Fred, Silvia and the boys had just returned home from visiting Jenny. It was almost six months since Billy had passed away.
The boys Archie and Joe had just taken their suitcase full of dirty clothes into the kitchen. Silvia their mother, said, "Just leave then on the floor, I will see to the washing later" and turning to her husband said
"How do you think your mum looks Fred?" I am a bit worried about her; she isn't coping very well since Billy died"

Fred Potts sighed deeply, he knew his mother wasn't coping she wasn't managing very well at all. His fathers passing had left a giant hole in his mother's life, a void that would be difficult to fill. He answered his wife.

"I don't know love, they were together for a long time, he did all the important things concerning paying bills and maintenance of the cottage, it will be hard now for mum to take over the role, she has only recently got over all the paperwork concerning
Dads Death certificates and her widow's pension" Fred took a deep breath.

To his way of thinking, his mum shouldn't have had all this stress, not so soon after the death anyway.

"I just don't think mum should have had all this to do Sylvia, not yet; it's too cruel"
The last thing a grieving person wants is to be bombarded with red tape, not at such a sensitive time. Silvia nodded in agreement. She had lost both her parents in a motor accident at the age of three, that was years ago, she had been brought up by her Grandmother, and remembered very little about her parents, she had a vague recollection of being on her mothers knee during a train journey, she remembered the fur collar tickling her nose, but that was all she could recall about her mother, but it may have been a dream, the memory was hazy. Neither had she any recollection of grieving for her parents.

But as her Gran was still living and had been resident in a retirement home over Dulwich way for a number of years. Silvia had had no dealings with death, but she would nevertheless miss Billy, he had been a wonderful man and the boys had clearly loved their Granddad.

She poured boiling water into the teapot, made a couple of strong cups of tea, and handed one to Fred. As she did Sylvia spoke.
"The boys seemed to enjoy the holiday love, but there is sadness about them since Billy died; and I must admit it was hard to come to terms with your dad not being there. Did you notice the amount of time Archie and Joe spent in the garden, I actually heard Archie talking to one of the gnomes?" Fred nodded. and answered.

"Yes I did love, they loved their granddad, and it is very apparent that they also have taken on liking the gnomes. Dad was potty about his (Little chaps), as he called them

"He painted um every winter; "They like a new set of clothes" He used to say"

"But to be honest Silvia; it didn't appeal to me at all. Dad was a bit eccentric, and if painting his gnomes gave him pleasure who was I to argue?" and it would appear the boys are following in their Granddads footsteps"

"Do you remember back last year when the boys came back home, after staying with mum and dad during the school holidays, and the dreams Archie kept having about Garden gnomes?"

Silvia thought for a moment. "Yes I remember; but I didn't pay much attention .at the time; Archie is always dreaming, he takes after your dad for that, it's hard for them to come to terms with his death, and you know they didn't want to leave their granny"

Silvia gave a deep sigh, "I'm worried about your mum being on her own. Do you think she would like to come to us?" Fred shook his heads.

"No love you know mum hates London, she can't stand the traffic, she isn't used to the noise and she says the pollution gets down her lungs"   Silvia knew what Fred's answer would be, but she couldn't think of a solution to Jenny's plight. They say time is a healer; but Silvia was concerned for her mother-in law.

They kept in touch by phone, letter, and a visit when they could. Then one day out of the blue came the solution to their problems. Fred came home from work at the solicitor's office where he worked as chief clerk.

"Silvia, sweetheart, BILBOW &DOBBS, are opening a branch near to mother's, about three miles from the cottage, and they have offered me the post of Chief clerk, what do you think?" "Oh Fred that's marvellous, our prayers have been answer

the boys will be absolutely thrilled" This was true, They both loved their time spent at the cottage, and had often talked about living there. The holidays had always been looked forward to. They didn't care how many times their mum and dad went off exploring different parts of the world, holidays to them was trekking around places like Nepal or Outer Mongolia. Their dad loved exploring weird and wonderful places, Joe being the eldest thought their mum only went to please their dad , He had heard her tell Granny that she went to keep the peace. He remembered Granny telling her to start pleasing herself for a change.

"If you don't want to go to these outlandish places Silvia; then tell Fred, he is a dreamer like his dad. Tell him you prefer Devon, you loved that holiday last year I remember you saying"

This was true. Silvia had loved the little harbour at Brixham. Her dream was to live down there when they retired. But due to the death of Billy, and Fred being made Manager of the Branch in Brenton, A move to the Cotswolds was on the cards. So Silvia would have to put any thought of moving to Devon on hold for now.

Plans were set in place, the house in London was sold, and within a further six months. Fred, Silvia, and the boys were living in the Cottage with Jenny.

August had been a good time to move, the weather kind. Of course, Archie and Joe were over the moon, they were living in Granddads Cottage. It was lovely, but oh' how they missed their Granddad' and Granny seemed to be sad all the time, it wasn't the same, but at least they had the gnomes. Yes. They had the gnomes. Oh but it wouldn't be the same, not without Granddad and the magic.

Fred began work at the Solicitors, the boys started school in Brenton, and Silvia and Jenny got on with work in the Cottage. Jenny was relieved she had persuaded the family to move in with her rather than buy a property nearby.

"I don't see the sense in you buying a house, when this cottage will be yours anyway"

So after discussing the pro's and cons of living together, it was decided that the money from the sale of the house in London would be used to extend the cottage at the back creating a self contained flat for Jenny. This work was to begin in spring.

CHAPTER 2

DIGGING and PAINTING

The family were settling into living in the cottage, and the boys were enjoying their first school holiday since moving in.

"Just look at the size of that big digger Joe, isn't it massive?" The boys were playing in the garden copying the builders. Archie looked at his own smaller version of the JCB, with a big sigh, he said to his brother.

"I wish mine was as big as the builder's"

Joe answered, "It's big enough for you squirt" Archie retaliated.

"Don't call me squirt our Joe" Jenny, on hearing the brothers bickering, thought to put a stop to it before they started fighting.

"Now then you two, that's quite enough of that, how about some ice cream to cool you both down?" Jenny remembered Fred when he was young, ice cream had always done it for him' whenever he was feeling argumentative.

The weather was warm, the spring sun, still pale and low in the sky gave a promise of it being a nice day. Archie, eager to get cracking with his digger, said to his brother. "Let's get a bit closer and look at that big hole"

Joe, the elder of the two, answered his little brother. "No Archie, you know what dad said; it's much too dangerous" Why don't we go into the workshop, and see what we can find" Archie, stood quiet, and shook his head.

"Granddad said not to play in the workshop, besides its locked" Archie knew Granddads workshop was locked, because he had been to the bottom of the garden and had a look when they first came to live in the cottage.

Archie had wondered down to Granddads workshop on his own the first week they arrived, he often did, it was a special place to him. Granddad had loved his Workshop and who knows' perhaps he would see him painting his gnomes the way he used to? Archie had walked by the side of it, remembering the slide he and Joe had made last winter, and Granddad falling flat on his bum, when he tried to manoeuvre the slippery sheet of ice, and the laughter the tumble had caused, Archie remembered the laughter. Archie gave a sigh.

Joe spoke. "What are you dreaming about Arch?" hurry up; Granny is calling us for dinner" Archie, nodded to his brother, "Come on then' I'll race you" Both boys enjoyed Grannies cottage pie, they always did.

Silvia and Fred were both at their chosen places of employment Silvia, had managed to get a job as laundry supervisor, and Fred, Chief Clerk at the solicitors in Brenton.

Work to extend the cottage had been going on for almost a week, everywhere was
covered in dust, the workmen were cheerful, three of them in all. They seemed nice enough blokes, but Jenny wasn't sure about the one they called Jake. Something about him she didn't trust. To her mind he seemed shifty, always looking round the place as if looking for something to pinch. She may have been wrong, but Jenny usually had a nose for a bad un; as she put it. Yes' Jenny meant to keep an eye on him.

By now she was sick of the mess. The boys were becoming a handful. If she had told Joe once to keep out of cement, she'd told him a dozen times. His answer that he was clearing up after the workmen had fallen on deaf ears with his Gran.
"I don't want your truck bringing cement into my kitchen and dining room" Why don't you go and find Archie, see if

you can do something more interesting than trundling cement all over my floors and carpets?"

Joe, feeling fed up, did as his Gran had suggested. he found his brother in the garden, by the fishpond. Archie looked up and said in a rather wistful way.
 "Do you remember when we cleaned out the pond, and Granddad fell in and got told off by Granny for getting green slime all down his best shirt,?" Joe nodded and laughed.
"Yes I remember alright, Granddad got his shirt dirty wiping the gnome clean"
that was before I knew the gnomes actually came to life" I didn't believe you or Granddad until he told me the story," Joe pondered for a while. .
"Do you fancy painting the gnomes?" Its early summer; a bit late, but Granddads little chaps haven't been touched since he died. "Come on Archie, let's do it"
Archie feeling a flood of excitement, smiled at his brother.
" O K, we'll ask Granny if we can do some gnome painting"

Jenny was a little unsure as to whether she could allow her grandsons to touch the gnomes, never mind paint them. Since the death of Billy, nothing much had been done to the garden, and as for Billy's precious gnomes, they had just sat in the garden where Billy had placed them. She remembered lifting the one Billy called MOLAC from the old gardener's arms after he had died, and feeling a bit strange when she touched the gnome? She also remembered something else to do with the gnomes, a dream. A weird happening!! It must have been something nice? Because Jenny wasn't frightened of the memory, she had put it down to a feeling, but it was probably imagination, so she had dismissed the thought. She had put the (whatever it was,) where it belonged, in the back of her mind. After all there was really no need to be alarmed, Billy had spent many happy years taking care of the gnomes. he wouldn't like to think of Jenny being worried about anything involving his gnomes.

Billy had had a spot in the garden for each gnome. Jenny secretly had thought Billy a little eccentric' but then Billy Potts had been one awesome fellow. She could hear him now, in her mind, speaking about the stone gnomes as if they were children.

"They do like their own place love, they are creatures of habit, same as us" Jenny had smiled at Billy's remark. Billy was a dreamer. It had been the same every year, ever since she could remember; Billy had painted his (little chaps) as he called his Gnomes, every winter. The pantomime of Billy buying paint from the hardware shop in a variety of colours every winter had always tickled Jenny. But she had surmised a long time ago, that Billy's little idiosyncrasies could be excused.

Well Jenny decided that, yes, perhaps it was a good idea, after all, Billy was gone, and he would never again be able to paint his little chaps. She gave a wistful smile. They were always his Little Chaps, to Billy.

"Alright then, I don't see why not, they are looking a bit neglected now" Wait until your dad comes home from work, I will ask him to take all the dangerous tools and fertiliser from the shed, check the paint, the half started pots in the workshop must be dried up by now, when that is done, and then you two can start work"

Archie and Joe could hardly wait for their dad to finish his tea. The moment he put down his knife and fork and left the dining table the boys were urging him to open the shed.   Fred, who was rather tired after a hard days work told them to hold their horses
for half an hour while his tea went down.

Eventually, after what seemed an eternity to the boys, Fred stood up and walked out of the kitchen.

"Come on then lads: and giving Silvia a knowing wink. Let us go to the Workshop" and see what we want in terms of materials to do the job" They set off for Billy's workshop.

The boys watched their dad put the key in the lock. With a creak the door swung wide open. The boys peered inside. There it was' Granddads workshop, It looked the same, it smelled the same, but it wasn't the same. Everything seemed sad, the cans of
paint were standing neatly on the shelves, some had been opened. Fred noticed that, where his father had used some of the contents, and it was evident by the paint that had run down the side of the pot, and had dried hard, that Fred would indeed have to replenish supplies before the boys could begin the job of gnome painting. He took the pencil from behind his ear, licked the point. Archie, fascinated as to why his dad had done that, he asked Fred if the pencil tasted of anything! He remembered seeing his granddad do a similar thing with his own pencil and decided it must be a family thing!! Fred answered his son. ."It tastes a bit like coal lad, I wouldn't try it if I were you" He reached into his top pocket and pulling out a small pad, proceeded to made a note of how much paint he thought the boys would need. He must stop the habit of putting his pencil in his mouth! Kids don't miss anything. It struck Joes mind, how did his dad know what coal tasted like?

Fred interrupted Joe's train of thought. "The shops are shut now boys. We will collect the paint in the morning" Archie gave a sigh' he was getting into the painting frame of mind he didn't want to call it a day just yet. He wanted to stay in Granddads workshop a bit longer. There was a big bottle of something called thinners that Granddad had kept for cleaning his brushes in. Archie recalled asking his Granddad why it was called thinners. Granddads answer had made Archie laugh. "Well, its better than calling it Fatties"

Further Secrets of the Garden

His Granddad had been funny. Archie could feel tears in his throat. "O h Granddad;
Why did you have to die? Fred seeing the lad's sad look said to him.
 "Come on Son" I've got an idea,"While I get rid of all the tools and stuff, why don't you and Joe, go and fetch the wheelbarrow, I have thought of a good idea"
Fred, after checking just how much paint he reckoned would be required for the boys to carry on where his father had left off, giving each little chap a new outfit each, he followed his son's outside. Archie gave a sniff, swallowed the tears that were threatening again, and wiped his nose on his sleeve. He said in a faltering voice
"Come on Joe, I know where the wheelbarrow is"

Fred Potts felt sorry for the boys, especially his youngest. Eight years old was young to suffer such grief, Archie had loved his Granddad so much; in fact the boy was full of love .both boys were, but his youngest was the soft one.
Fred spoke again, "Come on boy; your mother is calling you for bed.

CHAPTER 3

WHEELBARROW AND THE PRECIOUS CARGO

The boys were awake bright and early the following morning. Fred was already down and enjoying his boiled egg and toast. He smiled at his son's. "I thought you wanted an early start?" come on, get your breakfast" Archie and Joe sat down to cereal and toast. When both boys had finished their meal Fred spoke to them. "Make sure you leave enough room for your treat"

"Before you start work boys, how about a trip into town. I thought we could go into the café, have an ice bun then to HARDY'S STORE where we can buy the paint required for the job" It was good to be doing something constructive at last, it had been hard on the boys. Wanting to play in the sand and cement was a boy thing. they had been told off quite a lot. recently. The boys were all for that. Fred felt better, he didn't like bad feelings between himself and the boys, besides, he remembered his own childhood.
There were times he knew that he had misbehaved, and as they say, Boys will be boys.
After the trip out, tummies full of cream cake, everyone felt better, and ready for the challenge. They arrived back at the cottage laden with pots of paint and new brushes.

Fred gave the lads a potato sack. "Put that smoothly in the bottom of the wheelbarrow, then push it to the garden, and very carefully pick up each gnome, and place it in the barrow, when you've done that, wheel the gnomes back here to me"

Fred watched as the boys manoeuvred the wheelbarrow gingerly along the path at the side of the shed. He watched with baited breath, as they rushed excitedly towards the garden. Would they manage to do the job without breaking anything? Fred doubted it!! But he could hope. He

followed a few yards behind watching the wheelbarrow sway precariously from side to side his eyes glanced upwards, and with a chuckle to himself' thought. Never in the reign of Sam will they manage to get the gnomes back to the workshop intact; Fred couldn't see the gnomes making the journey without some being damaged, and that would never do. He caught up with them. "Steady on?
You're not running a marathon. Now then, leave the barrow by the path, and very carefully pick up one gnome at a time and place it on the sack"

The boys made their way towards the first little chap' Archie recognised the face, it was the gnome called MOLAC. He instinctively felt that he mustn't say the name in front of his dad, there had been a secret concerning the gnomes, something had happened not long before granddad had died, something so magical that he, and Joe had been sworn to secrecy, it hadn't been too difficult, because a soft spell had been put on them both. But he was remembering things now. Archie wondered if Joe was feeling it too.

He would find out when he was alone with his brother. He placed MOLAC in the wheelbarrow. After almost an hour all the little chaps were on the sack and being wheeled carefully to the workshop. by their father. For after the pantomime of the boys pushing the wheelbarrow, here, there and everywhere!! . Fred had suggested, it would be better for him to be in charge of such a precious load.
"After all boys, we don't want to break any of Granddads little chaps do we, they meant such a lot to him?" Joe and Archie nodded in solemn agreement.

.Fred thought that was a very diplomatic way of getting round the delicate situation.
of who should push the wheelbarrow, he knew the boys, and he had no desire to put their noses out of joint.

The precious cargo arrived at the Workshop. "Now Lads, if you go inside, I will pass the gnomes one at a time, and you can put them on the work bench"
As he spoke Fred noticed a shadow of something, or someone move from behind the workshop, there was also a slight rustle of debris as though someone had stepped on dry leaves, he stopped for a moment and listened, perhaps it was a rat, or a big bird..
His instinct told him that a rat doesn't leave a shadow. But there had been something.
Fred shook his head and concentrated on the job in hands. He wouldn't say anything to the boys. .
Joe and Archie did as their dad said. One by one, the gnomes were placed carefully on the flat surface. When the job was done there were twenty-one gnomes in all.
Fred said. "Listen lads, I can hear your mother calling us for lunch, come on, you can start to paint the gnomes afterwards"

Joe, who was fired up to start painting right away said.
"Do we have to go for Lunch Dad, I'm not hungry yet?"
"Neither am I " Said Archie, who was very keen to ask his brother something in private.

There was another call from Silvia. "Do you want cold food? now come on at once?" The boys traipsed into the cottage behind their dad.

"I thought corned beef hash was your favourite meal boys, especially when your Gran cooked it?"

Archie smiled at his mum she was right, he loved his Grannies cooking," It is Mum, but we just want to paint Granddads gnomes"

"Well, eat your meal and you can go back to the workshop and paint them after" I had better find out a couple of Granddads overalls though, otherwise it's hard to say where the paint might go, Get your oldest clothes on anyway, dirt seems to follow you two around whatever you're doing" The boys reluctantly got stuck into the hot meal, and it was noticed by their mother, that neither boy left a crumb of food on their plate. It was certainly a true fact that Jenny's cooking went down a treat.

When each boy had been fed, and suitably dresses in a pair of Granddads overalls by their fusspot mother, they set off back to workshop.

Joe began to laugh. "You look like the scarecrow in farmer Lambert's cornfield Archie"
Archie, feeling silly dressed in these uncomfortable daft clothes, thumped his brother on the arm.
"Shut up our Joe, and look at yourself; "You look stupid " Joe retaliated with.
"I am telling mum what you just said" We are not supposed to call people stupid."
As Archie went to give Joe another clout, Fred came round the corner of the workshop.

"Now what's all this shouting and thumping each other about then?" Granddad would be ashamed of you both"
"Now, are we painting gnomes, or are we going to lock the workshop and go to bed, it's up to you?"
Joe could feel his face getting hot. and Archie felt sad.
"Sorry dad, we want to paint the gnomes" Said the youngest brother, with a tremble in his voice, a tear in his eyes, and as if to make amends, he said to Joe.
"You pick the first Gnome Joe"

Fred Potts, feeling the tension between the boys subside and understanding at the same time that they were still both missing Billy. Put an arm around each boy's shoulder. It had been a very trying time for both boys. Their Granddad had meant such a lot to them, and they missed him so much, they were still grieving for the old gardener.

"Come on then, let's get cracking, He turned the key in the lock once more.
Archie wiped his eyes, and nose, on the turned up sleeve of the old overalls, he could smell granddad. Archie had liked that smell, a mixture of paint, bonfire, and oily rag. For a moment it made him even sadder, and he could feel another lump in his throat, but he didn't cry.

The boys were in the workshop. There were the gnomes, all twenty-one, inanimate, just standing where they had been placed before dinner. Fred spoke.

"Have you got a plan; decided how you are going to do the job?"
Archie and Joe looked at each other. Archie shrugged his shoulders, sniffed and blinked "Just paint um"

Fred smiled, and said. "Strategy boy's strategy" You have to have a plan" You have got to rub um down first, get rid of the old paint. Here, put these dusters round your mouth, keep the muck from your lungs" Archie yelled, "Do we have to Dad?" Fred, looking very serious answered the boys. "Yes you do. Mums orders"

Their father, trying to suppress a giggle, (well; the boys did look funny') "Have you decided on a plan of action?"

Joe put his finger under his chin in a thinking mode. "We could have a contest, see who paints the best gnome"

Fred answered the boy. "Why don't you get cracking on rubbing the old paint off first, then you can decide on how to go about giving them their new clothes, it's a good idea of yours Joe to have a contest," He was all for that, teach them that healthy competition was good.
(Fred was recalling his dad referring to the new paint job as the gnomes (new clothes). Fancy him remembering that?

"How do we rub the gnomes down Dad, do we wet them?"
Fred shook his head.

"Take a gnome in your hand, and with a piece of sandpaper, rub off all the loose bits of paint and garden dirt, then brush them gently with a soft brush, you will find everything you need in that old box behind the door, now get cracking; I will be back in a little while to see how you're getting on, leave the door open because of the dust, and keep those cloths round your mouth"

So feeling cluttered up in their oversized overalls and now the masks, the boys began the work of sprucing up the gnomes.

Fred left the workshop, and shaking his head, and smiling to himself, he wondered just what sort of mess he would come back to; He shuddered to think.

Joe taking charge, said; "Right Archie" "let's start with the best gnomes; .I bags, MOLAC" Archie bristled. You're not the boss anyway, I saw the gnomes come to life before you did, and you didn't believe in them then, it's not fair?"

Joe. Not wanting to give up the importance of being in charge. Said, "I'm the eldest, so I am the leader, you go and get one of the others, they've all got to be done so what's the difference?"

The difference to Archie was that his Granddad had died with Molac in his arms; this particular little chap had been his Granddads favourite.   Archie felt he had known MOLAC best. After all, he was the Gnome who had wiggled his bum at him, before all the other gnomes came to life, and before anyone else believed him that MOLAC had moved.

Archie appealed to his brother, "Oh please Joe, let me do MOLAC; I love him the best; and I know he likes me. Joe gave an exaggerated sigh...

"Oh go on then, you big baby" and not wanting to be out done by his younger brother, said.

" I'm doing LAGREN then, cos he is really the boss gnome"

And so began the task of rubbing down and painting the gnomes, it was going to be a long job. Archie picked up his chosen gnome, and with the sandpaper he began to rub the paint on the red jacket, as he did, he looked at the little gnome's face, .MOLAC appeared sad, was that a dried up tear in the corner of his eye, it couldn't be? Archie continued to rub. Perhaps he was mistaken? The gnome wasn't alive any more. How could he be?

Archie remembered the secret party last august, when the magic GNOME BEAM
 had brought all granddads gnomes to life. But he had seen them all go to sleep again after the party, never to wake for a hundred years.
He remembered standing by the side of granddads grave and promising to love the little chaps, so they would come alive again in a hundred years time.

Archie turned to his brother. "Do you think MOLAC has been crying; only I thought they went back to being stone after the GNOME BEAM had gone out after the party?"
Joe took hold of MOLAC, he turned him this way, and that way, he looked intently into the gnome's eye, and in his big brother voice.
"Don't think so, it's probably bird muck, just wipe it with a bit of rag" Archie did as his brother suggested, but to him, it still looked like a tear... not bird poo! Archie thought Joe was wrong, but he didn't say any more. He carried on rubbing the jacket with sandpaper. After about an hour the boys had rubbed down almost half the gnomes. By this time they were both feeling dusty and dry.

Joe, removed his mask, Archie started to laugh. "Your mouth is clean, but the rest of your face looks like its been in mum's flour bag" Joe sniggered," What about you, your white hair makes you looks like a ghost, and smiling said"
"Come on lets go and get a drink"

The boys walked down the path and into the kitchen. "Can we have a drink of quash Mum"   Silvia stopped ironing, and turning to the boys, she said.
"I think by the looks of you both, you had better call it a day as far as rubbing down the gnomes is concerned, just for the time being anyway. Take off your overalls and wash your hands while I get you a drink"

Silvia smiled at the boys, and turning to her mum- in –law "don't they look a sketch, covered in dust and flecks of paint from the gnomes, , Jenny nodded her head in agreement, but surmised doing that job had kept them out of mischief and out from under her feet. Jenny was also more than happy. The workmen were clearing away the tools and finishing the last clean up before they started work indoors.. The job of building the outside extension had finished, at last, weeks of dust, rubble and frayed nerves had come to an end. Best of all horrible oily Jake wouldn't be making his presence felt for much longer. It was reckoned by the Boss builder by the name of Trevor a chubby little Welsh builder, that they had broken the back of the new build' and the inside would only take a matter of a couple of weeks.

Jenny didn't like, or trust the particular builder called Jake, but supposed she could put up with the man for a few more days knowing that the end was finally in sight.   It was to turn out that her assumptions had been correct. Jake was a bad un alright.

The boys drank thirstily. The fizzy drink hitting the spot. Archie asked his mum
"Can we go and do a bit more rubbing down?"   Silvia shook her head.
"No boys, not today, it isn't good to be in a dusty atmosphere for too long, give it a rest for the time being. You've got plenty of time before you go back to school next week, why don't you go and give your dad a hand in the garden before tea, the fresh air will do you both good?"

Archie, arms by his side, head bowed, slumped out of the kitchen door. Joe followed.

"I don't fancy gardening do you Joe" The older boy shook his head.

"Let's go to the pond" see if we can get any frogspawn" Archie agreed. They walked along the path and around the back of the workshop. The gnomes were more or less where the boys had left them, except for MOLAC Archie looked through the workshop window. The Gnome in question, appeared to have moved closer to the window, and seemed to be staring out, still in his lifeless form, but there was definitely something different about him.

Archie mentioned it to Joe, but the older boy dismissed the idea.

"You must have left him there this morning Arch, the gnomes can't move by themselves anymore, not now the magic has gone" But Archie wasn't convinced by his brothers reasoning, besides; there was something else. MOLAC had a strange look on his face, and it was nothing to do with bird muck, and it hadn't been there when they had left earlier today!

The boys went to the pond, but Archie couldn't drum up much interest, normally he enjoyed messing about in the water, but he wanted to get back to the gnomes.

He knew there was something funny going on; But what? Was MOLAC trying to tell him something? Archie knew there was a special bond between himself and the gnome. He vowed to find out for himself, no matter what Joe said, he was worried for the little chap. There was definitely something different going on since they left the workshop this morning. Archie was right. But little did he know that his dad had been aware of a presence lurking around the workshop this morning, and MOLAC had seen the evil culprit.

Time spent at the pond, for Archie, was worse than having his toe nails cut, and he hated that, his mother always went too close to the skin with the scissors, Archie felt sure she would clip one of his toes off one day! He wanted to get back to the workshop. There was something wrong with MOLAC;

CHAPTER 4

THE THUNDERSTORM AND THE FLOOD

Unfortunately, for Archie, he wouldn't be going anywhere at the moment. except back to the cottage, for as the boys left the pond intending to defy their mother, and go back to rubbing down the gnomes, there was a loud clap of thunder, the sky's opened and the biggest storm they had seen for some time unleashed it's fury Soon the garden was swamped in water. The brothers, dashed to the cottage.
Silvia greeted them at the door, gave them a towel each." Come on, Lets get you out of those wet clothes, and into the bath " Granny is just running the water for you" We have been expecting a storm for some time, And smiling, said." Your Gran said she could feel it in her bones"

Archie, removing his wet clothes, had a sudden thought. MOLAC didn't have any bones, but was the gnome feeling something in his stone body brought on by the heavy thunderstorm. Perhaps a spark of electricity had switched on the tiny amount of Gnome Beam left deep inside allowing it to emit a surge of life? The boy was correct in his assumption as he would find out shortly.

Another clap of thunder seemed to rip the sky apart. The lightening flashes when they came were awesome, if a bit scary; Had MOLAC been aware of the oncoming storm, and was that why the gnome looked so different, sort of scared?

The deluging downpour of torrential rain and thunder had continued its havoc far into the night, and it was still raining at the moment. This meant both boys were unable to carry on with rubbing down, and painting the gnomes. So they decided, for the time being, to get the LEGO out of the box under the stairs, Archie had begun to build a tower earlier in the week, he would try to drum up some enthusiasm and carry on with that. Joe was more into his REMOTE CONTROLLED MONSTERS, and the new COMPUTOR GAME that was all the rage at the moment. But secretly Joe preferred his MONSTERS, the scarier the better. He especially liked the ONE EYED CYCLOPS. He was horrible, and to be honest, it gave Joe the creeps. But he wouldn't be admitting that fact to anyone.

However, after a while both boys became bored, they wanted to get back to the workshop. Their mum seeing them fed up, said" I know what you can do, Why don't I find you some paper, you've got coloured crayons ,how about drawing your gnomes and giving them different outfit, it would give you some idea of how to paint them when you can get back to them?"

Both boys thought it a good idea, so after putting everything else away, LEGO Back in its box, Computer switched off. They began crayoning gnomes, it wasn't the same, but it had been a good idea. Archie had imagined the gnome he was drawing was his friend MOLAC. The green trousers and blue jacket looked good. He would paint MOLAC in those colours. Joe had gone one better, his gnome was crayoned in rainbow colours. Archie thought that most unsuitable for a gnome!
Silvia seeing the gnome drawings- came up with an idea.
"How about crayoning your gnomes in different coloured outfit, then you can see which one looks the best"
The boys agreed with their mum, but to be honest-.they just wanted to get back to the workshop.

It was still raining hard. Fred, their dad had voiced concern about the brook at the bottom of the garden being in danger of flood.
"If the rain keeps on like this love" he'd said to Silvia and his mum. "I can see there being big trouble"

Jenny had agreed. "Do you remember Fred, when you were about the same age as the boys, the brook flooded out onto the field at the back, and Farmer Lambert lost most of his sheep and a couple of cows?
Fred nodded, "Yes I do Mum, and by the looks of things, we're in for something similar"

Archie overhearing the conversation between his parents and Gran, wondered if the memory of that occasion was anything to do with why MOLAC was looking so worried; After all he was very' very old, MOLAC and the other gnomes must have seen many changes during the hundred years. Had something similar happened to bring about the look on the face of MOLAC? .Joe could dismiss the idea as rubbish if he wanted to, but Archie realised there was something bothering the little chap and he must find out as soon as possible what it was.

Eventually the rain began to ease- it was two days before School started the summer term. Not much time to carry on getting the gnomes ready for the garden. At this rate the flowers would all be out before the little chaps were put back. Finally the rain stopped and the boys were relieved to be able to get back to the job of rubbing down, and painting the gnomes.

They set off, once again wearing the ill fitting overalls, and now Wellington Boots!
The garden was sopping wet, they needed boots to protect their feet. The brook at the bottom of the garden had flooded- water was everywhere, as they reached the path which sloped round the side of the workshop, both boys stopped. Archie piped up with
"Where's the path gone, we need a boat" He glanced towards the workshop window and to his absolute shock and surprise MOLAC was standing right up to the glass, and their for all to see were real tears running down his red cheeks.

Archie- without further ado plunged into the water- and screaming to his brother,
"I told you our Joe- I told you there was something wrong with MOLAC; But you didn't believe me;" Archie, spluttering, and gasping for breath struggled towards the workshop.
Joe could see with his own eyes that something was very wrong with the gnome.
He plunged waist deep into the water that covered the path, Archie being the smaller
of the two was wading through water which on him, was armpit high.

Archie reached the door of the workshop first, but he was unable to open it. Joe right behind his brother, shouted- "It's no good Arch- If we try to open the door, water will pour in" Archie struggled round to the window and peered inside, and with a gasp-
"Its too late Joe-water is already covering the floor" Archie glanced at MOLAC.
If a gnome could show fear, then it was evident on the face of the gnome.
MOLAC was actually shaking with fear, dust from the recent rubbing down swirling around him, the relief on his face at seeing the boys was most evident.

Joe looked at his brother. "What's happening Arch?" The gnomes are not supposed to come alive for another hundred years, we had the Gnomebeam Party last August just before Granddad died, they are supposed to be back in their stone bodies now, not crying and trembling like MOLAC is. Archie shook his head. "I told you something was wrong didn't I, but you didn't believe me did you" Again the youngest brother began to cry?"

Joe believed Archie now, he had to- for a start, and you only had to look at MOLAC to realise that something had gone very wrong. Joe signalled his brother to keep as still. as he could. He was able then, to reach around Archie and with a strength that came from somewhere, he managed to reach the lock, and prise the door of the workshop open.

The boys gazed about the place. The water on the floor was halfway up the legs of the workbench- lapping and swishing as they moved around.

"Look Joe" Archie gestured towards the tabletop. Archie could hardly believe what he was looking at.

All the lesser gnomes, so called because they had been made later than MOLAC

and the other five, had moved from the place where the boys had left them and now seemed to be clustering around the edge of the work bench; and to the horror of both Joe and Archie' one of the little chaps was on the wet floor. Archie, distraught, cried out!

"Is he dead Joe?" please don't let him be dead" Joe being less sensitive than his younger brother, said, "Don't worry Arch, how could he be dead if he isn't really properly alive? Archie retaliated. "How did they move then, you know where we left them before the thunderstorm; and it wasn't at the edge of the table?" Joe rolled up his sleeve, and reached down into the water, and picked up the lesser gnome, as he did so one of his concrete arms fell off, along with his hat.

Archie cried out, "Give him to me Joe; please let me hold him" Joe handed the wet now disabled gnome to his upset brother. Archie held the gnome gently.

"Get his arm Joe and his hat" and almost in the same breath "Do you think we can stick them back on?" The older brother shrugged his shoulders.

"It's hard to say" after all he's been in the water for a couple of days, and he's made of concrete, not stone like the better gnomes, and don't forget; we don't know where granddad put the magic glue when he stuck LAGREN'S thumb back on when we had the Gnomebeam Night Party, and besides, we don't know how to do it, I suppose we could ask dad" But that means letting him, and mum into the secret"

Further Secrets of the Garden

This of course was quite true. Their mum and dad knew nothing about the Secret of The Gnomes; how could they? When the awakening had taken place last August, they had been away on holiday, doing what they did most school holidays; trekking around some outlandish place or other, last autumn it had been Outer Mongolia for five weeks. They had collected Archie and Joe and gone back to London,. The boys had gone back home, vowing to keep the secret of the gnomes. It had been quite easy, as the soft spell put on them by the Keeper of the Gnomebeam, had prevented them from remembering too much about the fabulous extravaganza that had taken place in Granddads garden last August.

Billy for his part had never understood this gallivanting about! It had never made sense to Billy Potts. He had asked Jenny why their Son and daughter-in-law preferred foreign climbs rather than holidaying in England. Jenny had never understood either!
All Jenny Potts knew was that, every holiday the grandchildren had stayed with them.

She hadn't minded one bit when Billy was alive, he had loved the boy's .and always managed to keep them occupied. She worried now though that since her husband's demise, there wouldn't be enough to keep the boys occupied. But she was wrong. For little did she realise at this point in time, that this, was where the boys wanted to be. For since the awakening of the gnomes last year, and all the magic involved, and the big secret, this was the best place on earth to live. So Jenny needn't have worried. For it wasn't long after Billy's death that Fred and Silvia had sold their house in London, and moved lock stock, and children into the cottage. Of course, Joe and Archie thought the move was all part of a wonderful plan, an exciting plan that involved the gnomes. The boy's were quite right, for unbeknown to them they were part of a plot which involved the Gnomes, a magic trip, encounters of unimaginable wonder. But that was some way off. They weren't quite ready for the magnitude of such an adventure just yet.

Archie thought about Joe's idea of telling their mum and dad about the gnomes.
But he was against that idea. So as grown up as he could, the younger brother said.
"We made a promise Joe never to tell the secret of the garden, not to anybody, and a promise is a promise, we must keep it" and dismissing the idea, said " Why don't we dry the lesser gnome, put him in a plant pot with his leg and hat and think about what to do about the problem later"

Joe agreed, that was a good idea. After all, the lesser gnomes weren't really as important as MOLAC and his brothers.
 MOLAC, LAGREN, and the other stone gnomes had been hewn from rock by the old Bavarian peasant many years ago and given magic powers, as for the lesser gnomes, so called because of the concrete mix that made them, hadn't as yet been given the magic power in full. The old Bavarian gent had informed Algernon Potts that in time, if the love continued down the years, then the lesser gnomes would gain enough power to walk and talk almost as well as their more superior brother gnomes.

Archie whispered to his brother. "Do you remember on Gnomebeam night, when the lesser gnomes were trying to walk?" Joe nodded, yes he remembered alright. But still to him, it had been some sort of dream. He was finding it hard to come to terms with all this Magic stuff. Even more so now, for according to the story the gnomes weren't supposed to come to life for another hundred years, but here they were ten months on after the awakening and the Gnomebeam Night Party, still showing evidence of being alive. Something must have gone wrong with the magic spell!!

CHAPTER 5

THE GNOMEBEAM KEEPER AND THE BOX ON THE SHELF

Well it so happened, that nothing was wrong, The Gnomebeam keeper, was very wise. This was the first time since the magic begun, that children were involved in the Gnomes welfare. The Keeper of the Gnomebeam, decided in his wisdom, it would be better to allow a small amount of Gnomebeam to stay close to the gnomes. The keeper knew children didn't always get it right. Joe and Archie Potts weren't the first children he'd had dealings with. Oh no' The Keeper remembered way back in time, when he'd been called to a similar incident in a land far beyond the stars. But that was a different story, suffice to say, there are many planets apart from our own world that sustain life. Life that isn't too dissimilar to our own. The Keeper of the Gnomebeam knew them all. Children were children where ever they came from, some of the youngsters he'd had dealings with, came from far away planets, in different galaxies. Places as yet undiscovered by man who lived on the planet Earth. But Keeper knew of these worlds. Oh yes Keeper knew, and one day, a certain pair of brothers would also know in part. Not everything though, for no human mind would be able to take it all in. Keeper had plans for Archie and Joe, an adventure so fantastic that he felt sure they would find awesome in content. But that would come along later.

Keeper was also aware that a certain builder by the name of Jake Wilmot .wasn't to be trusted. Keeper was wise, he had been watching this man ever since work to extend the cottage had begun. He had watched Jake eyeing up the gnomes when he thought nobody was looking. But Keeper knew, Oh yes Keeper knew that that particular fellow was up to no good, and one day very soon, all would be revealed. Admittedly the builders had almost finished the work of extending the cottage. But one certain gent was out for mischief before the build was complete.

Archie's idea to put the disabled lesser gnome into a plant pot to protect him from any more damage had been approved by his brother. The boys also decided that it would be a good idea, to move the rest of the little chaps up onto the shelf that ran around the wall at the back of the workbench. The shelf in question had a lip in the front. Granddad had made it that way, there was also a little wooden box with a lock and key, attached to the inside of the lip, sort of secret. Archie remembered his Granddad being a bit strange, when he'd asked what was in the box. ."Nothing for you to worry your head about lad, it's just a bit of private paper," Archie had been there when the job was being done, he remembered his granddad, patting the wooden box gently and blowing his nose rather loudly. Archie had noticed before, that his Granddad always blew his nose, when there was something peculiar going on, but that time Archie could have sworn Granddad had had a tear in his eye.

"Don't concern yourself about the box." He'd said, as he returned to the business of the shelf. "The lip stops the tins of paint falling off" he'd told the lad as he hammered the piece of wood in position, and the box wasn't mentioned again.

So the job of moving the gnomes to the shelf began. First the tins of paint were moved together in order of colour. Red in one line, blue in another, and so on, eventually, a large enough space was cleared to allow room for all the little chaps. One by one, each gnome was given a place on the shelf. First the lesser gnomes were moved, it was a mystery how they had managed to get to the edge of the workbench from the position the boys had left them two days earlier? Best to get them settled first.

As the boys worked, lifting the gnomes onto the shelf, Archie reached over the lip and felt for the little wooden box, it was still there. What was it hiding and why had Granddad been so secretive about the box, and did Joe know of its existence?

Archie would have to find out.

The lad was just about to turn his attention back to MOLAC. When there was a call from their Gran.

"Come on you two, Dinner is on the table, you can finish what you're doing when you've eaten"

Archie shrugged his shoulder's he didn't want any dinner, not yet anyway. He knew it was one of his favourites, Pasta bake with mince, and baked beans, but MOLAC was more important than dinner. Archie was concerned about his little friend, he loved MOLAC. Perhaps it was because he'd been Granddads favourite, Archie couldn't say,

all he knew was, that at the moment, there was something going on that shouldn't be, and he was worried.

There was another call from the cottage. "Archie, Joe; how many more times must I call you, now come on at once before dinner is ruined"

The boys arrived at the kitchen door they had almost had to swim up the path by the workshop. Jenny took one look at her dripping wet grandchildren. This was beyond a joke. In a voice; that was far too quiet. Jenny spoke.

"Out of those wet clothes before you set foot in my kitchen; what with cement from the building sight being tramped in; builders nosing round, knocking on the door every five minutes asking for cup's of tea; and now you two with flood water up to your necks. I've just about had enough"

Silvia who had this minute come home from work, on hearing the commotion, came into the kitchen.

"Do as you're Gran say's and get out of those wet clothes, thank goodness you two will be back at School next week"

Silvia was also feeling the strain, she was in full agreement with her mother what with the three builders, in and out of the cottage, tramping cement and mud all over the place, the one called Jake, being especially overbearing, asking questions and being nosy. Silvia had voiced her concerns to Fred about that particular man. But he hadn't seemed concerned.

"Jake is just a bit brusque that's all; probably fed up with the kids and their tractors and diggers all over the place getting in the way of the work." He smiled at his wife. "Don't fret love, they have almost finished , I was talking to the little Welsh bloke, he reckons another day will do it and they will be away" Silvia had listened to Fred,: but she wasn't convinced, to her way of thinking, there was something not quite right about that particular builder. It would turn out at a later date; that her suspicions were correct.

But Silvia did agree with her mother. The children did seem in a permanent state of muddiness, or they were complaining they couldn't go out to see to those blessed gnomes. It had all been too much, even for her.
Luckily the swollen brook that had caused flooding at the bottom of the garden had begun to subside. Unfortunately however; it left in its wake a muddy rather smelly residue, this state of affairs helped to compound the already filthy conditions.

Fortunately, to almost; everybody's relief the outside of the extension was completed. .The boys wouldn't have minded the outside work continuing for a while longer though; they enjoyed the yard being full of machinery, piles of sand and gravel, it was smashing. But they realised the work had to come to an end sometime.

Now it was the inside. That would be very boring for Archie and Joe. No chance of running tractors and diggers up sand piles inside the house. Oh well' they had exciting; secret jobs outside, in Granddad's garden and Workshop.

Jenny Potts was dreading the upheaval of her home being turned into what she termed A bombsight. Silvia could understand her mother's frustration. The kitchen was her domain, and of late it had been like a Battle ground.

Silvia, trying her best to placate her mother, said
 "Never mind Mum, Just think what it will be like when its all finished, the cottage will be a palace, Fred was talking to one of the builders yesterday, he said another day would do it" Jenny sighed, and sent up a silent prayer, she wondered what Billy would have made of all the alterations. She half wished she had never agreed to this extension.

The boys had cleared their dinner plates. Archie moved his chair noisily on the gritty kitchen floor. "Can we go back to Granddads workshop, Please Mum?" we've eaten all our dinner" Silvia sighed, "You two and that workshop- go on then, but get your overalls and wellies on first, and be careful"

Archie and Joe didn't need telling twice, quick as a flash they were outside in the yard.. Jake who had just come round the corner, shouted after Joe and Archie in a gruff rubble voice.
 "I expect you two are off to paint the gnomes then?" Joe nodded, but he didn't speak, Joe didn't like Jake either. The boys made their way to the workshop. The water that had been chest high in Archie's case-was now down below his knees. Joe held his nose, "What a stink"
There was a smell of rotting veg, Joe didn't like veg at the best of time, especially cabbage, and that was what the smell was like, rotten cabbage Yuk!!

CHAPTER 6

MOLAC AND THE WORRY

They reached the workshop. As the boys passed the window, Archie yelled out,
"Look at MOLAC Joe, he's slumped down in front of the widow, looking at his boots, now tell me there isn't something funny going on?" Archie waded to the door through the smelly water, pushed it open and struggled through the stinking slimy mud that was clinging to his ankles.
"MOLAC, MOLAC, Whatever is the matter?" Archie could feel a lump in his throat. He took the gnome in his arms.
 "What is it MOLAC?" You've got to find a way to tell me."
Joe who was by now coming round to the idea that the gnomes were still alive,   whispered to his brother "I'm gob smacked Arch, absolutely gob smacked" You were right all along"

Archie feeling rather grown up, that his elder brother believed him at last took charge.

"What do you reckon then our Joe?"   Joe shook his head, "Can't make it out, can a stone gnome be worried, cos he looks upset about something?"

MOLAC was indeed very upset. He was remembering back to an incident many years ago, when he had experienced a similar storm, to this day he recalled the devastation caused to his blackbird friends by the torrential rain cascading down on the nest, he had watched helpless as the torrents of rain had washed the blackbirds nest full of baby chicks out of the ivy bush, he had watched helpless as they were washed away by the swollen brook. It had happened shortly after the first Gnome Beam night Party almost a hundred years ago, and MOLAC had- had no wish to see that happen again. He remembered one of the babies being washed by the water onto his boots as he stood immobile in his place in the garden, he had been unable to move, or offer any help. That sorry incident had scarred him forever. MOLAC would never forget the sad affair.

The trouble was. A similar situation had presented itself recently, in the shape of a Summer Storm. Another pair of Blackbirds had built a nest in the ivy bush, which was situated to the side of the workshop. MOLAC had been keeping his eyes on the nest from his position in the garden. Everything had been fine coming up to the Awakening, The magic Gnomebeam had gradually brought him and the other gnomes to life because of the ongoing love of the Potts family, he had been able to check on the blackbird nests, by hobbling over to the tree and looking up into the branches and listening for the chirruping of the chicks. But now, because the Gnomebeam had gone, he, along with all his brothers, had been turned almost back to stone. Meaning that, once again this year's baby birds had been in danger from the storm. MOLAC had been worried all over again, and he still didn't know if they had survived, and the way things were going-the power of the Gnomebeam almost gone. MOLAC felt absolutely useless.

Archie looked into the face of his friend, whatever could have caused the gnome to be so upset? MOLAC had a look of utter defeat in his eyes and Archie, turning to his elder brother. "What do you think Joe, there must be something the matter with MOLAC" There just has to be, look at him?"
Joe, pondered for a moment, he had an idea. He addressed his troubled brother.
"Put the gnome down on the workbench exactly where we found him broth" Archie intrigued, did as his brother asked.

Joe, with an air of authority, spoke. "Now Arch, if MOLAC could see, where do you suppose he would be looking?"
Archie thought for a moment before answering Joe.

"Towards the ivy bush I guess, said the younger brother.
"Hang on then little broth," said Joe, "I have an idea" with that, the lad opened the workshop door and stepping outside onto the watery path. Joe made his way, very gingerly towards the ivy bush.   Archie, puzzled by his brother's actions, watched as Joe pointed towards something hidden in the bush, Joe shouted,
 "It's a blackbird's nest, lovely and dry considering all the rain we've had. The chicks must have flown by now," With that Archie watched his brother feel into the nest. "Look" shouted Joe, "Dry straw and chick feathers"

The next thing that happened startled Archie.   MOLAC made an audible dry sounding noise and as the lad watched in awe. The worried gnome with a grinding sort of noise lifted his head from his boots, and gave a grin. Archie saw two teardrops well up in the corner of the stone gnome's eyes.   The transformation was unbelievable MOLAC was in his solid state, but he was actually moving weeping- and smiling at the same time. Albeit rather more robotic than Archie remembered, from the past.
Archie gestured to at his brother to look at the now, happy gnome. Joe gazed in absolute awe, and asked his brother.
"Was that the reason why he was so upset?"   But how would that bother MOLAC?" What has he got to do with the birds?" Joe shrugged his shoulders again. ." Don't know and what's more- how can we ever find out, but all I do know Arch," is that something put a smile on the gnome's face, and it was something to do with the birds nest and the chic feathers?"

Well- there was a way the boys would find out about that particular little mystery- but it would come much later on down the line as they travelled on this magical unbelievable, and mind blowing journey.

CHAPTER 7

PAINTED HEADS

The boys continued the job of settling the gnomes on the shelf. As yet, because of the weather, and having to stay indoors, the boys had only been able to rub them down.
Archie had pinned his crayoned drawings up on the wall of the workshop under the shelf that supported the gnomes. Joe was leaving his in the bedroom. "The paper will get damp in the workshop" he'd said to Archie. But Archie said he was leaving his there anyway.

It was decided, that as the autumn term was about to start on Monday, the boys only had Sunday left to start painting the little chaps. So not wanting to miss out, the boys got up very early, and after hurriedly scoffing their Cornflakes and toast, they rushed back to the workshop.

Joe placed the key in the door-turned it and the pair stepped inside. Everything was as they had left it yesterday. The paint pots were in the corner of the shelf, the gnomes were taking up the rest of the space standing erect and waiting.

Archie stood quietly. And turning to his brother said "Does it feel different to you"
Joe nodded in agreement- you couldn't put your finger on it, but the workshop felt strangely at peace. Archie felt the hairs on the back of his neck stand up. He felt Wonderful, what had happened to bring about this warm gentle feeling?
Neither boy could fathom it. Archie said in a whisper. "Do you think its something to do with MOLAC being happy?"
Joe shook his head." Don't know, but anything's possible in Granddads workshop, but I suggest we get on with the job; we only have today left before we have to go back to School" "lets mix the paint first"

Joe, being the tallest, lifted the heavy paint pots carefully down from the shelf and placed them on the workbench. Archie meanwhile began to sort out the brushes

When this was done, and Joe had put some thinners into a jam jar, he remembered

Granddad saying "You have to make sure you have enough thinners," its spirit to clean your brushes. Archie had wondered why spirit was called thinners, he remembered when Granddad had been alive he had pointed out." Well, it's better than calling it fatties" Archie still didn't know why it was called by that daft name. But the jam jar full to the brim with the (stuff,) was placed between them. Being filled to the brim was to prove a very bad move indeed.

Joe began by lifting two of the lesser gnomes down onto the work bench, and turning to his brother asked- "Do you remember the colours we crayoned?" Archie- in triumph, pointed towards his drawing pinned on the wall under the shelf. "There's mine, I told you to pin yours to the workshop wall as well"

I'm starting with MOLAC- I already know what his colours will be." As Archie prepared to begin, Joe rushed back to the cottage to get the crayoned masterpiece

from the bedroom. To Joe's mind his painted gnome was going to be the best.. He ran upstairs, and as he did, his mother shouted after him.

"Don't forget its School tomorrow, don't stay out in that shed too late this afternoon, it's a bath for you two, nails cut, hair washed and an early night"

Joe answered his mother.

"O K Mum". He didn't mind the bath, but he simply hated having his hair washed- his mum rubbed too hard, and, she got soap in his ears.

Joe ran back to the workshop, the path to the side was still very wet, but the water. had gone almost back to normal. He opened the door. MOLAC was standing resplendent in bright blue trousers and the beginnings of a green jacket. Joe-secretly thought his young brother was making quite a good job of the paintwork.

But he reckoned his own would be better. So with no further ado, he pinned his own crayoned work up on the wall next to his brothers. He compared the two pictures. To his minds eye his own red picture was the better of the two;   Joe began to dip his brush in the pot, which contained the red paint and began with painting his chosen gnome's trousers a brilliant red. He carried on quietly; he was going to do the best job. After a while, Joe looked across at Archie. MOLAC was very handsome; he would have to watch out, his younger brother was doing a fine job!! He would have to do something about that!! So accidentally on purpose. Joe flicked a blob of the paint onto Archie's neck. Archie, who had been busying himself quietly for about half an hour looked up startled.
."Why did you do that our Joe?"   Joe shrugged his shoulders, and answered .his brother.
"You looked miles away, I thought I'd wake you up, anyway you've taken up all the space on the workbench"
Archie bristled. "I have not, we both have the same, you big pig, I'm telling mum about you"

The workbench was indeed a good size, allowing both boys as much space as was required. Archie had glanced across the bench to where his brother was working studiously a little earlier on, and thought to himself, that Joe seemed to be very serious in his painting. So the splat of red paint had come as a shock. Archie couldn't understand why his brother would do that?

'But Joe hadn't thought to mention to Archie that in his mind this was a serious contest as to who would do the better job? Joe at the moment; thought Archie was making a good job of painting MOLAC- and that would never do, for he had determined to himself that he would be the winner and do the better job- so he must do something to make sure he won. Very sneaky!!

As Archie concentrated on the green jacket, he hadn't noticed his brother coming round the workbench towards him. All of a sudden, splat' a big red blob of paint landed on the side of his neck. Archie jumped up. "What was that for?"   There was another splat, this time down the side of his face. Archie white with temper, stood up.
"You rotten pig, I'll get you for this, with that, his brush was rammed to the hilt into his tin containing green paint. Smack' Joe received a blob of green paint to the back of his head; the paint ran slowly down his neck and into his overalls.   Archie mad now!! Stuck his green brush into Joe's red paint and proceeded to wipe it all over his brother's hair. There was such a hullabaloo; hollering and shouting, .that Jenny heard it from the kitchen. She rushed outside and made her way to the workshop. When she arrived, Jenny stopped in her tracks appalled at what was before her.

"WHAT IN THE BLAZES IS GOING ON HERE" The boys, on hearing their Gran, and realising what they were in for, stopped what they were doing, Joe especially feeling guilty and rather hot in the cheeks, because he had started the paint fight in the first place. He didn't know why he had done it, and judging by the angry look on his Gran's face Joe wished he hadn't.

"Just look at the pair of you. What in the name of justice do you think you're playing at?" Good job your mum and dad have gone for a long walk" Jenny was furious with her grandchildren.
 "How on earth you expect me to clean up this mess, Heaven alone knows"
"Get to the cottage at once before I skin you both alive, and don't go inside until I figure out what to do with the pair of you. Do you understand?"

The boy's shamefaced and paint splattered slunk up the path. . Jenny looked at the mess in the workshop. Paint all over the floor, and the workbench was ruined,   Billy had kept everything so nice, what would he have thought of all this? Under her breath, she uttered "Fred and Silvia will go absolutely mad"

She locked the ruined workshop, and followed the boys.
 She was trying in vane to remove the paint with hot water, soap and lard, when Silvia and Fred walked through the gate. Fred shouted out.
"We could hear the commotion down the lane, what on earth is going on here?" Both parents stopped in their tracks. In front of them was the answer. There was Jenny red faced and fuming, and the boys stripped to their underpants, standing in the old tin bath full of hot water, being covered in lard, scrubbed and shouted at- all at the same time.

Fred, said in a voice seething with quiet anger, "I'm waiting for an answer boys" Jenny, with the scrubbing brush on the back of Joe's neck, carried on furiously trying to remove the paint, Joe at the top of his voice howled
"You're hurting Gran, I'll have no skin left" and in a screeching voice shouted Mum, get Gran off me. I bet my neck is bleeding"

Silvia stepped in to the furore. "Now, let's all try to calm down, and going towards the tin bath, she looked at her sons in dismay.
"We have to get rid of the paint from your skin, if we don't, you could be scarred for life" and taking the brush from here mum, she carried on scrubbing at Joe's very sore, but not' bloody neck.

Fred, watching the brush go back and forth on his son's neck; exploded with anger.
"It's no good doing that Silvia, turps is the only thing that will shift gloss paint" With that. Fred Potts went hurriedly

towards the workshop to get a bottle of spirit. Silvia stopped scrubbing, everything went deathly quiet.

All of a sudden there was a loud yell from the bottom of the garden. Fred had reached the work shop- and opened the door.
In a further thunderous roar- he yelled-
"I can't believe what I'm seeing- the place is ruined, absolutely ruined, Just you wait till I get back up there to you two " Silvia could never remember in the years she and Fred had been married, ever hearing him so distraught, she didn't think he could shout so loud.

Fred arrived back with the turps, white faced and angry. The boys, still standing in the tin bath, held their heads down when they saw the look on their dad's face. Jenny, who by now was feeling calmer, tried to placate her Fred.

"They didn't mean to cause such a mess Son, we can soon clean it up"
Fred came towards the boys carrying the bottle of turps. "Get out of there the pair of you- put these sacks around your shoulders, 'I'll try and remove the paint with this"
Fred held the smelly turps in front of the boys. Silvia, feeling concerned about the flammable liquid being used on the boys, said.
"Be careful Fred. I don't like you using that stuff on the boy's faces and heads it's much too dangerous"

Fred tried to dab, dab very carefully with a small amount of turps, but it was no use,
For one thing, the smell was horrible, and another, he knew Silvia had been quite right; using the turps on the boys faces was potentially lethal. It had been a bad idea.

Jenny feeling it was too much for the boys, made a suggestion. "Why don't I go and run a nice hot bath for Joe and Archie. I am sure we can wash a bit more paint off with

nice bubble bath, then we can decide how to remove any left, besides, its almost supper time now"
The boys, feeling relieved that the smelly stuff wasn't going to be used, climbed out of the tin bath, and rushed almost naked to the cottage, and upstairs to the bathroom. They were both soon into the nice warm and sweet smelling bubbly water. Relieved that ordeal in the tin bath was over. Jenny did her best with a soft flannel to remove the remaining, offending paint. But try as she might, there were still areas of stubborn green and red paint refusing to budge.

She felt a little calmer now, and realised that yes! She had been a little heavy handed with the scrubbing brush. But she had been at her wits end.
The job done to the best of her abilities, and the boys dressed in their pyjamas. Jenny prepared a warming meal and as they sat down to enjoy the tasty hotpot, the atmosphere that had been frosty, relaxed once more.

But it still remained that the boy's hair was covered in red and green patches of paint,
and it was school in the morning. Silvia came up with the final and only solution to the painted heads problem.

"There's only one thing for it, and that's scissors. The painted hair will have to be cut off" .Silvia looked towards her youngest boy. She was still angry, but all the same she felt a little sorry for the predicament they now found themselves in. Her boys would have to attend school in the morning, with by her reckoning, at least half their hair missing. Silvia sighed.

"Archie come on, I'll cut you're hair first" The younger brother looking like it was the end of the world, sidled up to his mother. Silvia gave her boy a smile.
"Come on love, it's the only thing to do" we've tried everything else, it won't look too bad and there's   one thing certain, your hair will grow again"

Archie sat on the stool in the kitchen, his mum put a towel around his neck. Snip, snip, pull with the comb, a few yells from Archie and the job was done.

"The mirror, I want to look in the mirror" Archie stood up and walked towards the mirror on the kitchen wall. Shock Horror"

"My hair, my hair, I've hardly any left, you've scalped me Mum" Archie was horrified by the image before him. Most of the hair from his head, apart from a ragged tuft right on the top had gone, there was a wisp sticking out from above his right ear.   But that looked stupid, especially with the bald head still showing bits of red paint, he felt with a trembling hand gingerly round the back of his head, here and there he could feel bits of hair sticking out of his scalp.

Archie could feel tears of humiliation welling up in his eyes. "I can't go out like this, and I'm not going to school tomorrow either" Silvia, answered her son with as much authority as she could muster..

"Oh yes you are Archie, it's the start of the new term, you must attend, besides' your hair will grow in no time. Silvia turned away from her son's accusing stare. He did look rather odd, and also dare she say comical- but she mustn't t laugh that would be rubbing his nose in it, .she felt sorry for him never the less. But she hoped that the painting each other episode, had taught her boys a valuable lesson in common sense.

Every action has a consequence. The sooner they learned that valuable truth the better it would be.

Now it was Joe's turn for the scalping. He had looked at his brother's new Hairstyle with trepidation he sat on the stool, and as Silvia placed the towel round his neck, he screeched   "Don't cut my hair as short as Archie's Mum, cos he looks daft. I'm not going to school tomorrow with him looking like that"   Silvia tapped him on top of his head with the comb. "You are both going to school in the morning even if I have to drag you there myself, I can assure you both that you look equally silly, so get used to it perhaps you will learn from this little episode not to be so inconsiderate to each other in the future, now sit still" Silvia mustn't let the boys see that inside she was weeping silent hurting tears.

Snip, cut, snip, went the scissors. Soon there was another pile of painted hair on the floor, and Joe had a new haircut.

He looked in the mirror. He was completely bald on the left side of his head, he still had most of the other side, and some of the top, perhaps he had faired better than Archie, having kept most of his hair, but he did look a sketch. Silvia finding it hard to keep her composure, smiled at her funny looking son. "It will soon grow Joe.
Don't worry"

The two boys eyed each other up, Archie laughing at his brother, shouted "You look like half a Mohican, and proceeded to do the Indian war dance round him, .hollering and whooping smacking his hand to his mouth, Joe angry now, shouted back "Well you look like the other half. Before Silvia Jenny and Fred could stop them, the angry brothers were rolling around the kitchen floor.
With no further ado Fred grabbed both boys by the scruff of the neck and hauled them to their feet.
"Now that is quite enough, what is the matter with you two?" I don't think either of you realises just what a mess you've left me to clean up in the workshop; the sooner you both get back to School the better it will be" and don't think you will be allowed back in the workshop until you can prove to your mother and me that you have changed your ways"
Archie piped up "But Dad we have to go back and paint the gnomes, they need to be back in the garden. Granddad always put his little chaps back in the garden freshly painted in spring, and it's summer now, they've got to go out"

Fred gave a sigh of utter frustration "What did I just say lad?" you should have thought of that before you caused the mess?"

"As far as I am concerned you and Joe have marked your cards good and proper, so until I see some improvement in your behaviour, the workshop is out of bounds, and I don't want to hear another word about it, do you understand"

The tears that had been threatening for some time, began to well up in Archie's eye's,

With a quivering lip, and head bent in shame at what he and Joe had done, Archie whispered "Sorry Dad"

Fred Potts looked down on his son's almost bald head, patted him on his shoulder and with a lump in his own throat said.

"Go on lad, and just remember my words " Fred watched as his son walked towards the cottage, shook his head and sighed, that little episode had hurt him far more than it had hurt the boys, perhaps one day his son's would realise for themselves just what it cost to be a parent.

CHAPTER 8

BACK TO SCHOOL

Silvia had been in contact with the Head Master of WILLOW DEAN SCHOOL.
She had warned Mr Taylor about what had occurred to the boy's hair during the holidays. He had comforted her with assurance that he would ask his staff to keep an eye on the situation, make sure they weren't tormented by the other children too much "Boys will be boys, Mrs Potts, try not to worry," he'd said. But Silvia couldn't help
being worried. The boys looked comical; there was no getting away from that fact and despite knowing that the situation they were in was their own fault, Silvia felt sorry for her boys.

"Some kids are cruel "she'd said to Fred. "Can't they stay home until the hair grows a bit, Silvia could feel herself weakening from her resolve to teach them a lesson. " I don't want them bullied?"   But Fred had been adamant. "No Silvia, they have got to learn to face up to problems, not shy away from them, it will stand the boys in good stead for the future, after all you know as well as I do that life isn't one big funfair"

So after dressing in their uniforms, making sure their normally hated School caps were snug on their bald heads, and only half eating their breakfast, the boys caught the school bus on the corner. Silvia waved them goodbye and let loose the tears she'd been holding back.

She arrived back at the cottage. Jenny met her at the Gate. "They got off alright then love?" Silvia nodded, unable to speak owing to the lump in her throat, after a moment.
Silvia answered.

"I hope the boys will be alright Mum, cos you must admit they both looked very odd?" Jenny put an arm around her daughter-in law. "They will be fine, try not to worry besides the hair will grow back in no time at all, and they have learned a valuable lesson they are not likely to forget in a hurry." But little did either parent realise it wasn't only children who could show a nasty streak in their nature as Joe and Archie were about to find out.

Miss Archer, the maths teacher, who was taking the first lesson after morning assembly looked through horn-rimmed spectacles at the children in her class.
Miss Rosamond Archer was a battle axe. A middle aged biddy, she had no real liking for the children in her charge. Tap-tap with her ruler on the desk, and in a thin, pinched voice "Quiet, all of you, quiet I say" Her beady eyes alighted on the Potts brothers.
 "Stand up the pair of you, Caps must not be warn in class, remove them at once" Archie and Joe stood at their desks, arms by their sides, caps firmly on. Miss Archer drew in a deep breath Tap-tap again with the ruler on her desk.
"Caps off at once" Miss Archer had been made aware of the painted heads incident, all the teachers knew about the unfortunate happening. Most had chuckled, seeing the funny side of it, .and vowing to make light of the situation. Not Miss Archer though, no, not the maths teacher. She had decided to make an example of the Potts boys.
"REMOVE YOUR CAPS AT ONCE"- You could have heard a pin drop, every one of the twenty five children were silent. From somewhere at the back of the classroom somebody broke wind, a loud resounding explosion. There was a titter amongst the rest of the children.
Miss Archer, white with rage, stood up, and fixing her eyes on the boys, who were seated a couple of desks apart, shouted through clenched teeth "Come to the front of class - NOW"

Everyone was quiet. There was a scrape of chairs, as the brothers left their seats. The boys walked slowly towards the battle axe. Archie and Joe stood before the monster. Miss Archer opened her mouth.

"Well- and what have you got to say for yourselves, and come closer?" The boys did as they were told. Joe noticed the teacher's teeth were a greeny yellow colour, and she had some missing. He shuddered. Miss Archer was ugly: The teacher, a glint of spite in her eyes, grabbed both caps at the same time "I'll teach you two to defy me" As she tugged at the snug fitting head covers, Joe yelled out, both hands trying to prevent the cruel deed- "No Miss, you can't"   But she could, and she did. As the caps were forcibly removed, a strange thing happened. As Archie and Joe were standing in front of class feeling vulnerable, and embarrassed heads bare and bald in places.   The classroom suddenly erupted with clapping and cheering. A voice from the side yelled,

"Three cheers for Joe and Archie Potts"

The noise of Miss Archer shrieking at the children to sit down was drowned out by children congratulating the brothers for having the nerve to turn up at School looking so ridiculous.

Miss Rosamond Archer was last seen running out of the school gate never to return.
Her cruel taunt had backfired, she had turned the boys into Hero's and not objects of ridicule. Was there a lesson to be learned here? Probably! The one that says Good will triumphs over evil.

When Silvia, Fred and Jenny heard the story about what happened at School, Silvia and Fred went to Willow Dean School, determined to have a strong word with Miss Rosamond Archer. But on arrival they were informed that the lady no longer worked there. Apparently, it had been expected for some time that Miss Archer, would eventually go too far.

Mr Taylor had informed Mr& Mrs Potts with the facts, when they had gone to the school to complain about the treatment doled out by the maths teacher.

"Well it's like this" said the Head Master." Miss Archer had been the topic of concern for some time we have been keeping a weather eye on her erratic behaviour, fearing that the woman was heading for a breakdown, and I am sorry to say we were correct in our assumption, Miss Archer is being cared for at the TIDEWAY MENTAL HOSPITAL which is situated on the coast, after she suffered a complete breakdown"

Silvia; quite deflated now from any feelings of anger. Offered the Head Master her
commiseration's. After a few more words about the welfare of her children, and being assured that nothing like that would ever happen again, she and Fred left the school.

It was now September. Fred was busily trying to clean the Workshop after the devastating paint fight between the boys during the school holidays. He still couldn't work out what had possessed them to do such a thing? It wasn't like them at all.

Could it have been the weather, heavy rain and flooding keeping them indoors? It had rained rather a lot of late, and he knew how much the boys enjoyed being outdoors.

The brook had gone back to normal now, so the path by the side of the workshop was clear, if covered in silt like mud. Fred had done his best to get the workshop back to normal, there were still some stains on the workbench ,they would never come off' But he had got it back into shape after the paint fight. He noticed the gnomes had been put neatly on the shelf above the workbench, they had all been rubbed down, and apart from the two that had been painted before the paint fight, they were now waiting to get their new clothes.

Fred smiled to himself, he was remembering his Dad refereeing to his little chaps new clothes, Every winter it had been the same, his Dad Billy, sitting out in his work shop painting his gnomes a new set of clothes. The newly painted little chaps were put back in the garden exactly where they came from. "Every little chap has his own place in the garden, it's the same every year, his Dad had said, "They like their own place lad" Fred hadn't really understood his Dad's reasoning? But he had put it down to a little eccentricity on the old man's part.

Gradually over the course of a few weeks the boys had both grown a new head of hair, during that time Fred had relented his anger towards his sons, and Archie and Joe were allowed back in the workshop on the strict instructions that nothing like the paint fight should happen ever again.
Unfortunately, because of the weather, and the boy's misbehaviour, the gnomes, for the first time in years had been unable to go back in the garden, they had been stuck in the workshop for months.

The boys, determined to make up for their bad behaviour, were once again working to get the gnomes painted. It had been decided that, as the nights were drawing in, they would only be able to paint at weekends. Winter and dark nights would soon be here.

It was almost time for the builders to quit. Another couple of weeks should see the end of the job. The work on the cottage extension had taken longer than anticipated, owing to the flooding around the property, which had been unfortunate. Of course it went without saying that the family would be glad to see the back of the building sight, and the builders. Jenny especially, she had been the one having to put up rubble, dust, and men traipsing all over the cottage. Jenny would be relieved when she had the place back to normal. She would also be glad to see the back of Jake. Jenny was unable to put her finger on why she didn't like that particular builder? But there was something about the man that unsettled her. It would soon come to light, that she had been justified in her gut feeling of mistrust towards this man.

The family were pleased with the almost finished result. Two more rooms, downstairs cloakroom, and a good sized conservatory had given them the extra space needed.
There was only the clearing up to do then the workmen would be on their way. Jenny especially gave a sigh of relief. So while Jenny and Silvia pondered over curtain and flooring catalogues, wondering from the vast array of choice, what to choose. Fred organised the decorating.

Archie and Joe got stuck into the work with renewed vigour. As each Gnome was finished, they were put carefully into a large cardboard box, each one wrapped separately in newspaper for added protection. They would stay in the workshop safe, until next spring. It was unfortunate that for the first time ever, MOLAC, and the other Gnomes hadn't been ready for the garden this spring. But the boys made a determined effort that next year the Gomes would look the best ever. They would make their granddad proud. They really hoped he would be able to see his 'little chaps' from heaven. The boys felt pretty sure that was where Granddad was now.

They determined to finish the gnome painting job for definite. , the trouble was. With Bonfire night just around the corner' building the fire at the bottom of the garden, kept the boys busy. They had finished all but two Gnomes. Still to be painted with their fresh clothes, was the one called ABLEG and one of the lesser gnomes.

It had been decided by Fred and Silvia that being as the boys had towed the line since the (Painting each other incident.) They could have a bonfire party,
Being as it was their first year of living in the cottage. The boys could invite some of their friends to celebrate

November the Fifth with them. The boys had welcomed this. So Joe and Archie decided that the two unpainted little chaps could wait for a while. They could sit on the shelf in the workshop. There would be time after Bonfire night to finish the job, and they did so want a good garden party. They would finish painting the little chaps, and all twenty one must be in the garden in their own places for next spring. They absolutely must. But it wouldn't hurt to have a really smashing Bonfire night party!!

The boys had just finished their tea of fish fingers, chips and peas. Archie's absolute favourite. The Family had been discussing the (New Cottage,) 'That was how they saw the new build. The extension to the back had given the house a different feel, altogether.

The builders had finally finished. All that remained to be done in 'Jenny's Den' as the boys put it. Was to lay the new carpets and put the furniture in place. Jenny especially liked her kitchen. The window looked out onto the back garden. This had been Billy's domain. She would be able to enjoy reminiscing, what the garden had looked like when tended by Billy. She would of course enjoy what was planned for the garden later. It was a shame that the boys hadn't been able to finish painting the gnomes yet. But Jenny felt sure that, next spring, all the gnomes would be in their place.

Fred had finished putting the new carpets in place All the remained was to put the furniture in its new home.
Jenny spoke up. "Doesn't it all look nice" Fred smiling, answered his Mum.
"Yes it looks smashing, and with your titivating' the cottage will be a palace" Fred was well aware of his mother's eagerness to get the cottage into shape. She had hated the upheaval. But on reflection, he reckoned she had coped well.

Jenny did indeed quite like the new arrangement. She had never experienced seeing things from this angle. Fortunately, or perhaps unfortunately!! Jenny was about to witness more that she bargained for from her new kitchen window. Something very disturbing was about to take place.

CHAPTER 9

BONFIRE NIGHT

The time was moving on a pace, it was now the beginning of October. Fred, Silvia and Jenny had almost finished the clearing up and settling into the new way of life. The boys had thrown themselves into building the bonfire. It had been decided, that the bottom of the garden, where it had been built last year was definitely the best position. Billy had been very wise, the boys had asked last year why the fire was right down at the bottom of the garden. To be told by their Granddad.

"It's the safest place boys; far enough away from the cottage, to stop any sparks from igniting the thatch, and near enough to the cottage to hear when you're Gran calls me in for me dinner"

Archie remembered with sadness his Granddads words.

Joe, huffing and puffing, came round the corner pulling an enormous log of wood. Archie was following behind, with a couple of very smelly planks, attached to which was a load of chicken wire.

Fred met the boys by the now, rather large bonfire. When he saw what the boys were carrying, and got a whiff of Archie's offering. He said rather pointedly,

"Hang on boys; you can't put the wire on the bonfire. Where on earth did you get it from?" As for you Joe; are you sure you were given such a good piece of wood for burning" Both boys nodded, and Archie answered.

"Farmer Lambert gave them to us, he said he was having a clear out, and if we wanted, we could go back to the farm and he would find us some more bits and pieces for the fire"

Fred sighed and shook his head. That was very generous of old Rufus Lambert; but it was rather out of character.

Perhaps the old Farmer was going soft in his old age? Fred hoped that the next lot of kindling from the farm wouldn't smell so pungent, and it was a certain fact in their dads thinking, that when their mother got a whiff of the chicken muck' the boys would be in the bathtub being pampered with perfumed bubbles, before they could say 'Jack Robinson'

Fred surmised again about the timber being given away as rubbish by the Farmer. Some people have more money than sense.
But it would prove a little later on, that a sizeable piece of timber from Mr Lambert's farm, was to come in very handy indeed

The nights were drawing in now, and it was dark by about six p.m. the family had just enjoyed fish and chips, this was the usual meal for a Friday evening. Everyone agreed that Mr TUBBS served the best fish and chips in the whole of the area around the village of Barraby.
The boys had gone to bed. Fred was enjoying a cup of tea in the sitting room. Silvia and Jenny were washing the pots after the meal.

Jenny, tea towel in her hands, trying to peer out of the window, spoke to her Daughter- in –law,
"Did you see that Silvia?" something moved over by the gates" Silvia, not in the least concerned, answered her mother-in –law.

"It's too dark to recognise anything Mum you must have been seeing things" Jenny folded the tea towel and placed it over the rail in front of the new ARGAR and took a deep breath. She hadn't been seeing things. Silvia was wrong. Jenny decided to say no more on the subject and keep her thoughts to herself.

Jenny was just about getting used to the innovation of the new appliance, but she thought it slower than her own gas cooker. But she determined to herself that the monster cooker would be mastered very soon.

Jenny, however, wasn't convinced by Silvia's answer that there was nothing by the gate. She had seen what appeared to be two lights by the entrance to the property. Not clearly, but she had seen them, she may be getting on in years, .but her eyesight was still good.

The boys were doing their best to get to sleep, but due to the excitement of preparing for the bonfire party at the weekend, both were too wound up, they were talking about the evening, how many fireworks they had, and the supper of baked potatoes, and soup their mum and Gran were preparing for bonfire party. . Neither being aware of what was about to happen

Both boys were sitting on Archie's bed, which was situated by the window, when an arch of light could be seen creeping silently around the bedroom wall. Joe was the first to speak, he looked towards his brother.
"That's strange Arch, what do you suppose it is?" Both boys stuck their heads close to the window, and peered into the blackness outside……Nothing, not a sound, apart from a dog barking some way off.

They were awakened in the morning by their Gran calling them down for breakfast.
"Come on you two. Your boiled eggs will be like bullets if you don't soon get to the table. You don't want to be late for school, besides I have a lot to do today if you want a good party tomorrow night."

Both boys scrambled downstairs, eager to enjoy their breakfast, the lights they had seen moving round the bedroom wall last night…forgotten.

Silvia seated at the table, finished her cup of tea, and addressing her sons.

"Before you leave to catch the bus, there's a broken apple box by the door, take it down to the bonfire, it's a bit of extra wood to burn.
"You had better get your scarves and gloves on as well it's very cold out today"

The morning had arrived bright and cold there was a slight frost on the ground and a sting in the air as the boys hurried down to the bottom of the garden carrying the box between them, suitably clad in their warm but cumbersome attire.

As they passed the workshop, Archie noticed the door wasn't closed, he turned to Joe,
"Has Dad been down here this morning cos he's left the door unlocked?" Joe shrugged his shoulders. "How would I know, we've both come out together"?"

Archie went towards the workshop, as he did so there was a groaning creek and the door very slowly swung wide open..........In the next moment there was pandemonium.
In a high pitched voice, unrecognisable as belonging to Archie, the young boy yelled out,." MOLAC, MOLAC, Help Please help. Somebody has taken the gnomes, and in an even louder voice called out," Dad, quick Dad, all the gnomes have been pinched"

Silvia and Jenny hearing the commotion, hurried down to the workshop.
Archie in floods of tears met them. "Mum, all the gnomes have gone, every one"
Somebody horrible has pinched um!! With that the young lad was inconsolable.
With renewed tears Archie cried out. "MOLAC oh" MOLAC, Be brave, we will find you all soon"
 Joe from inside the workshop, shouted out "No Arch, not all of them, they've left ABLEG and one of the lesser gnomes behind" Then addressing his mother.
" What are we going to do now?"

Silvia, wiped Archie's tear stained eyes with her duster, it was the only thing she had in her hand, and trying desperately to console her youngest, answered Joe.
" We will go back to the cottage and phone the police, don't touch anything in the workshop Joe, they will want to look for finger prints, I am getting in touch with your Dad as well" With that Silvia, her arms around Archie, walked up the path with Jenny.

Both women were upset, who would do such a thing? Joe meanwhile was about to leave the workshop, when he heard a noise, it seemed to be coming in the direction of the shelf above the workbench. He listened again. What was it? Perhaps a mouse had found its way in, and couldn't get out, but Joe reckoned he had never heard a mouse make that sound. He walked towards the shelf and listened once more. In a rough gravely sound that came from where ABLEG and the lesser gnome were standing.
To Joe, the noise was like someone with the worst sore throat he had ever heard..
 There it was again. "J A K E- J A K E." Joe was sure the strange sound was coming from very near, he stepped closer to where he thought it was coming from.

Joe was standing in front of ABLEG, and the lesser gnome, and with a glance towards the gnome's faces, Joe knew, he just knew.   He was looking into the pleading eyes of ABLEG. Joe feeling absolutely gob smacked, addressed the gnome.
"What are you trying to tell me ABLEG?" Once again, the stony, rubble noise, that Joe realised was coming from the gnome, started to speak
"J A K E, it was J A K E.! M O L A C gone with bad man last night". And in an equally rough sandpaper voice the little gnome, inconsolable said. "Me so sorry, you find my brothers"

Joe was glad he was alone. Who would believe that a GNOME had told him who had done the dirty deed of

stealing the gnome's, or that a stone gnome could show such feelings and be so upset?
Joe tried to think. He wouldn't be able to tell his mum or dad what the gnome had said. So how could he tell them that he knew who had taken MOLAC, and the rest of the gnomes?.

Joe motioned to ABLEG, and the lesser gnome who also looked upset. For although   this little chap hadn't uttered a word, Joe could tell by his miserable demeanour that he also had witnessed the thief take the other gnomes. Joe tried to console the pair by telling them that he would do all in his power to get the gnomes back home. With that he made his way to the cottage.

When he arrived Silvia was speaking on the phone; "Yes it must have been last night officer; the gnomes were still in the workshop at about 9 p.m. when my husband went to check everything was alright" Silvia carried on speaking for a few more minutes.
"You say you will be here in about an hour then?"   After receiving an answer, she put the phone down.

Joe could see that his little brother was still very upset. His Gran was sitting with Archie, trying her best to console him. She had her arm around him and he was weeping on her shoulder. Joe thought for a moment. Perhaps he could talk to his Gran about ABLEG. After all she had been part of the AWAKENING PARTY last spring, when Granddad had still been alive. She hadn't mentioned it since then, but she had been there, he knew there was a lot of magic concerning the special Party, but although he remembered his Gran being in a sort of daze at the time, she must have been put in a similar soft spell as himself and Archie. But nevertheless she had been at the party, she must recall something.

Further Secrets of the Garden

Archie red eyed, looked up from his Gran's shoulder. "Mum's called the police Joe, and in a sobbing voice said. "But they won't find them. I expect they have been sold to a garden shop; we will never see MOLAC, and the other little chaps ever again?"

Jenny shook her head in dismay, and looked at Joe, how was she going to give a word of comfort to her youngest grandson? Joe feeling ready to burst with the news about ABLEG knew he had to speak to his brother and his Gran before the police arrived.

Joe sat down by the side of Jenny, and in a whisper he said. "Gran I must talk to you"
Jenny looked puzzled. "What about love" Joe motioned to her to come over to the window, out of earshot of his mother. Jenny, not knowing quite what was going on took Archie by the hand, did as Joe asked.

The older brother began. "Gran, do you remember the party we had in the garden last spring" Jenny looking nonplussed, stared at Joe. "Well I do sort of remember something love, but I am never quite sure when I recall that night, whether it was a dream or a real memory, anyway Joe, what has that got to do with the gnomes being stolen"

Archie at once seemed to perk up, and asked his brother "What are you asking Gran that for?" Joe realised that he had to tell Archie and his Gran, what he knew. But how would they take it? Especially, he wondered about his Gran's reaction to the tale.

As he began to tell the story of what had happened in the workshop earlier. Archie, in a most unusual show of affection towards his brother threw his arms around Joe's neck. Jenny, on the other hand, appeared completely dumb struck.

Archie, in a loud whisper said "You mean ABLEG saw who took MOLAC, he saw the robbers?" The young lad feeling real hope that something good was happening, said in a very excited voice. "Quick lets tell Mum" With that Archie, called out to his mother. Joe, quick as a flash, put his hand over his brother's mouth. "No Arch, we can't tell mum, don't you remember the secret"

Archie wriggled free, "We have to tell Mum and Dad, we've just got to"

Joe, knowing this couldn't happen answered his brother." If you tell them, the magic might go, we may never see the gnomes again and we will never ever hear them talk and move about; anyway ABLEG, didn't know where Jake had taken MOLAC, and the rest of the gnomes"

Silvia on hearing her son call out, answered him "What is it Archie" Jenny who somehow realised that Joe had been right, and there was indeed a special secret to keep. Shouted back, "It's alright Silvia, I will see to the boy" Then turning to Joe.

she said in a hushed voice. "Tell me later" Joe nodded back to his Gran.

There was a knock on the door, and at the same time Fred, who had just got home after being phoned at work about the theft, walked into the cottage, followed by a police constable.

Silvia greeted both, and recognising the Policeman, said "Hello Harry, how are you, and how is Susan" The Policeman removed his hat. "Fine thanks Mrs Potts, The missus hasn't got long to go now, the baby will soon be here, and chuckling said.

As long as she doesn't give birth tomorrow, don't want her going with a bang. Bonfire night an all"

Fred ushered the police officer to a chair. "Sit down and take the weight off" Silvia has just made a pot of tea" PC Harry Walters was glad to do just that. His corns had been rather painful of late. The constant pounding on his beat didn't do his feet any favours. Mind you, P C Walters, was rather rotund, he had an overindulgent fondness for his wife's home made fruit pies.

He took his note pad and pencil out of his top pocket.
"Now; can anyone tell me anything about the theft, has anyone notice anything unusual lately, a stranger perhaps, any one hanging about the property, heard any strange noises?" The family were quiet. Joe especially was relieved that the police man arrived when he did.

Fred was remembering an incident a while ago. He recalled being in the workshop, when the boys were busy getting ready to start painting the gnomes. He hadn't said anything to the boys, but there had been something odd. He addressed the constable.
"I do recall something, back when the house was being extended, when I was in the workshop with the boys; they didn't hear anything; but I did"
P C Walters put up his hand, "Hang on Fred; let me get this down on paper"
While this was going on, the policeman taking notes. Jenny was recalling the lights she had seen last night .from the kitchen window.

She spoke to the policeman; "When you have finished talking with Fred; I have something to say" When her turn came Jenny told of the lights by the entrance to the property late last night but she thought it better not to say anything about what she had witnessed in the workshop earlier. As she did so; Archie piped up, the lad was feeling much better now he realised there was still hope that his beloved gnomes would be found.

"We saw them as well Gran, lights creeping round the bedroom wall; it was a bit scary; but when we looked out of the window there was nothing to see, but we did see lights; honest we did"

P C Walters made an accurate account of all he'd been told, writing every detail down in his note pad. He asked at length about the extension, being built. He turned to Fred, "Can you give me the name of the firm who carried out the work" Fred went over to the kitchen dresser, he opened the locked drawer, he fingered through the papers. After a few moments, he found what he'd been looking for.

"Ah yes; here we are THOMAS BAINS and SON.

P C Harry Walters scratched his head. "Do they, by any chance employ a gent by the name of Wilmot, Jake Wilmot?" Jenny piped up, "Yes he was one of the builders, a cheeky blighter, sticking his nose into everything. I didn't like that one at all; there was definitely something unsavoury about the fellow"

The P C stood up, "Leave it with us, I thought it was about time Wilmot showed his hand again, try not to worry, you will be hearing from the station very soon, we know exactly where to find that slippery eel; I feel certain we will be able to bring this state of affairs to a satisfactory conclusion." With that the police officer took his leave.

It so happened that the police weren't the only ones to have their eye on Wilmot.
Keeper of the Gnome beam had been watching the goings on for quite a while, he had been aware of the builder nosing around the cottage ever since work had begun. He had waited his time, and now the time had come.

When P C Walters returned to the station with the news that Jake Wilmot had been on the building work at the cottage, it didn't take long for the police to put two and two together, it seemed they had been waiting for such a time as this. The man in question had been on the short list as being one of the robbers who had stolen garden ornaments from various places where reconstruction work had taken place. But up till now they hadn't been able to pin Jake Wilmot down, but this time, it seemed that their luck was in.

Archie and Joe couldn't wait to go to the workshop and tell ABLEG, and the lesser Gnome, that the police had all the evidence needed to arrest Jake Wilmot. But first they would have a word with their Gran.

On hearing the tale about the two gnomes telling Joe who had taken MOLAC and the others. Jenny insisted on going to the workshop with the boys to see, and hear for herself. Jenny had to admit, that the story seemed very far fetched. But in view of

the fact that there always had been peculiar happenings with the garden gnomes. After all hadn't her husband Billy always loved his little chaps, and hadn't he died with his favourite Gnome MOLAC in his arms? Treating them more like children than stone gnomes.

After telling Silvia and Fred that she was going to make sure Joe had left the workshop just as it had been left by the robbers. She accompanied her grandchildren to Billy's workshop.

CHAPTER 10

IT WASN'T A DREAM AFTER ALL

Jenny motioned to Joe to open the door of the workshop, reminding him not to touch anything. The three stepped inside. Archie, full of expectation, whispered to Jenny.
"Are you scared Gran"   Jenny squeezed his hand and said, "No not scared love, just intrigued"   ABLEG, was standing where Joe had left him, the lesser gnome by his side. Both of them just inanimate stone figures.   Joe walked over to the bench, and addressing the two gnomes. "Don't worry anymore, your brothers have been found safe" They will be home where they belong in a few weeks."   For a few seconds, all was quiet.
Jenny rather bemused smiled to herself. The boys seemed to be as daft as their granddad had been about the gnomes, treating them like friends rather than stone figures. But what happened next dispelled any such thought she may have had about all this being stuff and nonsense.

On hearing the good new, the two gnomes did a strange thing. ABLEG the larger of the pair, seemed to wriggle and move towards the lesser gnome. From his voice a lilting dusty; gravelled noise, almost like gruff singing; came from beneath his beard. The lesser gnome, eyes open wide and slightly crossed with the effort of trying to make himself heard,   endeavoured   to   move   towards   ABLEG. Unfortunately he was unable to do so. But Archie and Joe were certain they had heard a scraping sound coming from the direction of where the lesser gnome was standing.

Jenny; stunned by what she had just witnessed, shook her head in disbelief. And in a voice no more than a whisper said. "So it wasn't a dream after all" Jenny just couldn't believe her eyes.

The boys had given the little chaps some very good news and as far as Archie and Joe were concerned, the day that had started out so badly, was after all .turning into something rather wonderful. They could look forward to a smashing bonfire party after all. Archie moved towards his Gran, .who was in a state of shock. She hadn't moved since ABLEG and the lesser Gnome had made verbal and scraping noises.

He took her hand. "Come on Gran" But, Jenny still transfixed didn't budge. She looked at her Grandson. "They can talk and move Archie. It just isn't possible"

She seemed to come to her senses, and stepping towards ABLEG, she peered into his face, and asked quietly. "How can you be real?" What happened next almost made her jump out of her skin. ABLEG pulled himself up to his full height and puffing his cheeks out blew a mouthful of dust into her face, and smiling, said in his gravel voice. "Billy knew we were real, Archie and Joe know we are real; .and now, so do you"

It was five thirty in the evening, when the phone rang. It was from the police station.
Fred, who was just about to take a final look at the Bonfire, stopped to take the call.
"You mean you've got the blighter already; well that's excellent news, where was he Harry?"
Fred thought it was alright to address the officer by his first name, after all they had been friends for quite a while, In fact Fred had known the man since his school days, they had both attended the village school, anyway; since Silvia and Fred had moved back to Barraby, the friendship had been rekindled besides; they were both in local pub darts team.
The officer carried on talking for quite awhile. Fred listened intently to what P C Harry Walters was saying.
"We couldn't believe our luck Fred, The bloke could see us, but he just stood there with the box of gnomes in his

hand; he had started to run, but stopped right in front of us. To tell you the truth Fred, it was rather scary; almost as though some force was holding him back; almost like he had suddenly been frozen stiff; although when I got my hands on him; he felt normal" PC Walters stopped speaking for a moment; Then in a voice full of puzzlement, and at the same time shaking his head;…The bloke was muttering something about seeing a Dragon. "Funny that"

Well unbeknown to the police, this was exactly what happened. Keeper of the Gnomebeam, being fully aware of what had gone on, had trained the light onto the robber, so awesome was its power; that Jake Wilmot was held captive by its strength. So terrifying in content was the image before him that the builder would remember for a long time the dream that had been introduced into his mind. Dream like pictures that had scared Wilmot so much. But he would never be able to understand the full implication of what he had witnessed during the time he was held captive by the power of the Gnome beam.

The truth of the images would all be revealed at a later date, but not to the builder, and because the beam was magic, the police had been unable to see it either; Jake had seen the police; and had started to run. But Keeper; who was in charge of the Gnome Beam; so called because it was all part of the magic of the gnomes coming to life; was one step ahead of the robber, he had watched the villain take MOLAC and the rest of the gnomes from the workshop.

Fred, unable to understand either, was nevertheless thankful that the culprit had been caught red- handed. He thanked the officer and proceeded to inform the family about the good news.

He explained to the boys, that for the time being; the gnomes must remain at the police station as evidence of the crime; they would be returned in due course, after the trial.

Of course, Archie and Joe knew all about the Gnome Beam. They remembered it being part of the magic party last year; Just before their Granddad Billy Potts; had been found dead in his old cane chair with his favourite Gnome MOLAC; in his arms.

Billy had loved his Gnomes. The boys knew this. Archie especially had seemed to understand this special love his Granddad felt for his little chaps. After all Archie had been the first to see the gnomes move; he had witnessed MOLAC wiggle his bum when he and Joe were helping Granddad in the garden, while spending their School spring holidays at the cottage; before they came to live here, eighteen months ago.
Joe hadn't believed his brother; that he had seen the gnome wink and wiggle his bum. That was, until he had witnessed for himself; the gnomes moving and eventually talking.

Everyone was relieved that the gnomes had been found. Jenny because they had always been special to Billy, besides, she realised for herself now that there was something strange about the little chaps, they really could come to life; She had seen for herself. She sort of recalled something happening at a special party just before Billy had passed away, something to do with the Gnomes, but the event had always been rather hazy in her mind. But Jenny had always felt certain that whatever it was, had been nice. She remembered lovely music; she could recall pretty lights, and strange little Orb like beings floating about the garden; each carrying in their hands tiny trays full of food. She could also taste the fresh salad; if she really thought about it. But because she never came up with a plausible answer to the question of a strange party; Jenny usually dismissed whatever it was that occasionally came into her mind as stuff and nonsense. But now Jenny realised that now everything wasn't imagined, or dreamed. It was all true.

Anyway, that was quite enough at the moment. There was another party to see to; a real one and if she didn't look sharp there would be no toffee; ginger bread made or potatoes scrubbed clean for roasting in the Bonfire.

It had been decided that a few of Archie, and Joe's friends from school could be invited to the bonfire party. Six thirty on the eve of November the fifth, found five friends from school, accompanied by their mum or dad ; and in some cases both; All arrived at the Cottage within an hour of each other; fortunately the weather was ideal,
it being both cold, and calm.

The first guest's to arrive were Alan Firth and his mum, followed by Becky Rogers, and her dad. Ralph Rogers, an acquaintance of the family smiled as Jenny welcomed him. "Hello Ralph; nice to see you again; she smiled at Becky, and noticing the paper bag containing fireworks the girl was carrying; said," My oh my Becky; that's a big bag; you will make sure your dad lights them won't you ;?" The rather plump; red headed girl smiled and nodded at Jenny, rather unconvincingly. Jenny made a mental note to keep an eye out this evening for that little miss.

Jenny was remembering an incident last Christmas concerning this spoilt little madam. When at the carol service at St Steven's; this girl had caused mayhem by stuffing huge quantities of snow down the pan of the outside toilet. The said convenience was ancient to say the least; but the disruption caused by the large amount of compacted snow was rather 'inconvenient' especially to the vicar, who had suffered many troublesome years from the effects of an over active bladder, and needed the comfort of knowing the toilet was within reach at all times. The yellow snow was noticed by some of the parishioners, who were taken short, during church services; but nothing was said and eventually the snow thawed.

A few more guests arrived, eager to enjoy the party, and at seven thirty the bonfire was lit by Fred. Everyone waited with baited breath for the tiny flame to take hold of the straw and paper that had been packed inside the large stack. With cheers and clapping, especially from the grownups; the fire was well and truly ablaze Soon there were shouts of delight as yet another rocket soured into the cold night sky or a giant Catharine Wheel whirled round and round on its nail hammered into the garden fence, throwing out garlands of multicoloured sparks.

Archie and Joe were in their element, this was a smashing party, especially now that Jake Wilmot was out of the way, and more importantly, MOLAC and the other Gnomes were found and safe. The boys had discussed how long they reckoned the police would keep the 'little chaps' and had been quite happy when their dad had assured them that they would soon be back home to the workshop.

The evening was in full swing, everyone happily enjoying the occasion; Jenny's home made toffee, along with soup and rolls had gone down a treat with the guest's Fred had just put a dozen or more scrubbed potatoes into the red glow at the bottom of the bonfire, when there was a huge explosion, from the side of the cottage. Everyone ran towards the area, to be confronted by Becky Rogers, dishevelled and looking very frightened, running like a scared rabbit, towards them.

The girl was crying. Ralph Rogers was bringing up the rear, Ralph who was on the chubby side, shouted breathlessly at his Daughter, "Becky; what on earth are you doing, you could have been killed?"

Well when it came to light, the girl, unbeknown to her parents, had managed to get hold of a packet of bangers, she had swapped some of her pretty fireworks with a boy at School for some of his loud ones, despite being told by her parents, when she had asked, that these dangerous fireworks were out of bounds. Apparently she had tied two of the monster bomb like horrors together, and put them in the dustbin situated at the back of the cottage. On inspection of the dust bin; Fred found to his annoyance that the stupid girl had blown the lid clean off. He found it some distance away resting up against the wall of the workshop.

Ralph Rogers apologised for his daughter's bad behaviour, Becky traumatised by her experience asked to go home. Jenny's premonition about Becky had been correct. The party continued for a further hour, the children enjoying the baked potatoes judging by the charcoal mouths they all displayed, and after a few cheery choruses, where everyone joined in the singing, the bonfire party came to an end.

CHAPTER 11

THE GNOMES RETURN HOME

After the bonfire party, when everything on the fire was cooled down, Fred and the boys cleared the ash, put it into bags, Fred remembered his dad always cleared a fire and kept the ash for the garden ."It makes good fertiliser Lad "The old man used to say. Fred wondered idly what his Father would have thought about the saga of his gnomes being stolen and the exploding dust bin. Probably the latter would have brought a chuckle to the old man. The first incident would have made his blood boil. . His dad had loved the gnomes like they were his own children.

There was something else the boys had noticed, but they would keep quiet about this;.
Archie had gone into the workshop shortly after the exploding dustbin caper, he had gone at once to find his brother and inform him of what he had found.

Joe had followed his brother, to find ABLEG, standing guard over the lesser gnome.
Archie said to his brother, when they were both in awe of what was before them.
"Do you think ABLEG was trying to protect the lesser gnome when the explosion sent the dustbin lid flying into the workshop wall?" Joe nodded; "I'll bet that is just what happened" and scratching his head,
"Do you know something broth, these gnomes shouldn't be moving like this; there is something weird going on" Archie gave a sigh, and nodded to his brother.

About a week before Christmas Fred received a phone call from the police informing him that he could go and pick up the gnomes from the police station. Of course there was great excitement in the Potts household. Archie and Joe, busy in their room tying up Christmas presents for the family, where both in a heightened state of excitement. Joe was in the middle of wrapping a selection box for his Gran, she loved chocolate' when there was a cry from Archie. Who instead of sorting out which present was for who' was gazing out of the bedroom window.

With a yell, he shouted "Dads back Joe, he's just putting the car in the garage" In an instant, Joe was at the window; he shouted excitedly "look Arch, Dad's lifting a large box from the boot" With no more ado the boys were out of their room, and clambering downstairs.

Archie was first to reach Fred. "Have you got them Dad, is MOLAC ok?" Fred, puffed out from carrying the heavy load, said. "Hang on lad, this is a big box, full of homesick gnomes" course there're heavy. Archie smiled, his dad was a tease.

Fred proceeded to carry the heavy cargo to the work shop. Stopping as he did so at intervals to catch his breath. Taking his handkerchief from his pocket and wiping his forehead, he gasped to Joe and Archie. "Jake Wilmot must have muscles like Charles Atlas.! This is hard work for me and I am fit"

The box was eventually placed on the workbench. Archie, eager to see his gnomes, tried in vane to remove the strong tape that was securing the sides of the prison. Fred Who noticed his son's frantic attempts to get to his gnomes stepped in. "Get out of the way lad, let the dog see the rabbit" With that. Fred ran the blade of his pocket knife across the tape on top that was securing the cardboard box.

Archie and Joe, stood each side of the box, they pulled and tugged until they had opened the gnome prison. There they were; all the little chaps. Archie alarmed at what was before him. Spoke to his dad. "They should be stood up Dad! Looks like they've been chucked in the box any old how" Fred peered inside, shook his head. A pile of gnomes lay higgledy pigledy in the cardboard box. He would be complaining to the police station later. Good job his dad Billy hadn't been here to witness this.

Fred taking charge of the situation said "Come on boys, let's get the gnomes out of the box and check for any damage" And so began the task. As each little chap was lifted from the box, he was examined carefully by the three. Joe, on taking out one of the lesser gnomes shouted out, "He's lost an arm, and a bit of his nose" Archie, upset about this discovery, searched for MOLAC. He found him right at the bottom underneath his brothers. He lifted him gently. As he did so, the gnome gave a deep sigh and a whimper. Archie overcome, cradled MOLAC in his arms and whispered quietly "You're safe now he said to the gnome. "Don't worry anymore" Fred who had heard the sigh, said to the boys. "Did you hear that noise?" Archie and Joe had both heard it. But realising that Fred didn't know the secret of the gnomes, looked blank.

Both boys shook their heads. "No Dad, we didn't hear anything. Fred, thinking perhaps he was mistaken carried on lifting the gnomes from the box. They continued until every gnome had been lifted out and checked. They found only three little chaps had been damaged. Two of the lesser gnomes had limbs knocked off and poor KITRAM had lost an eye.

After all the gnomes had been placed on the worktop, Fred took his leave after telling the boys that he would try to fix the damaged gnomes the following Saturday.

Archie and Joe were relieved to be alone at last. "That was a close one" said Archie. Joe agreed, but he was wondering more and more now just how much longer they could keep the secret of the gnomes from their Mum and Dad. But the most important thing at the moment was that the little chaps were home, where they belonged.

The boys feasted their eyes on the gnomes, apart from looking a little dusty and shaken, they didn't seem too bad. Archie picked up MOLAC once more. "It's good to have you back, we've been so worried" As he did so, there was a humming noise coming from the direction of the shelf where ABLEG and the lesser gnome were standing. Joe and Archie cast their eyes in the direction of the noise. Archie, eyes wide open, stared as they watched the scene. They watched and listened transfixed at

ABLEG as he swayed back and forth, and at the same time a gravelled gruff melody was coming from his mouth.. The lesser gnome, standing close by seemed to be moving his head, if rather robotically, in time with the humming.

"Will you look at that Joe" said Archie to his brother. "I think ABLEG, and the little chap are welcoming their brothers home" Just then, as if on cue, the gnomes on the table began to hum. At the same time beautiful music could be heard. It seemed to be coming down from the sky.

Archie looked at his brother. "I remember hearing music like that when we were staying with Gran and granddad, just before Granddad died" and looking at his brother. "Do you remember Joe?" The older brother nodded, "Yes I do; but what do you reckon is happening?" Joe was recalling the story about the Gnomebeam only supposed to bring the gnomes to life every hundred years. "The thing is broth do you think something very peculiar is going on?" Archie looked at his brother, who smiling answered. "Don't know; but isn't it exciting?"

The humming and dancing came to an end, and as though it had never happened the gnomes were as garden gnomes should be, inanimate, and still. The boys gave a final check on the gnomes, closed the workshop door, locked it, and walked towards the cottage.

CHAPTER 12

THE BEST CHRISTMAS PRESENT EVER

Jenny met the boys at the door. "Come on dinner's ready, Your Mum and Dad have gone into town; some talk about last minute present's; Jenny thought privately to herself that enough money had been spent already; but she shrugged her shoulders, It was Christmas, and people always spent too much money on things that they could do without.

"Wash your hands boy's ; then sit to the table; its your favourite" Archie and Joe tucked into the cottage pie and peas, Archie, cheeks bulging, "I could eat this every day Gran" Jenny in mock annoyance, "Don't speak with your mouth full Archie"
How many more times must I tell you to chew your food" Archie, giggled, "I do Gran; But I can't wait to get the pie to my tummy; so I chew ever so quick" Jenny trying to hide a smile; "Get on with your dinner my boy,"

It was almost evening when Silvia and Fred came home. Silvia, sounding and looking warn out, kicked off her shoes, and began to drink the welcome mug of tea.
"Oh Mother; it was a nightmare in the shops; people pushing and shoving; kids screaming for this and that; Thank the good Lord Christmas comes only once a year.

Fred, for his part, was glad to be home; shopping never had been one of his favourite things to do. Glancing towards his son's, .he asked "Did you manage to sort out the gnomes?" Both together they answered "Yes Dad" Archie said" We put the bits of broken gnome into a plant pot, like you said" Fred nodded, "That's fine boy's; I will Take the glue down to the workshop in the morning before I go to work; .it shouldn't take long to stick them back together.

By now it was pitch dark outside; and snow that had been threatening for days was beginning to fall.   Archie and Joe decided that they would carry on making the castle started some time ago. They had over a period of time amassed quite a lot of Lego bricks, so the castle was going to be quite impressive when it was finished.

There was however one item that had been missing for some time. This was the Drawbridge, They reckoned, it had accidentally been thrown away, at some time, picked up as rubbish and thrown in the dustbin. It had been a useful piece of kit.
Dad had suggested they use a modified shoe box lid, it served the purpose, but wasn't really ideal.

Silvia called. "Come on boys; that's enough building for tonight; its school holidays, you've had extra time, now its bath time, and off to bed with you"

Archie, who was reluctant to stop the important building work "Oh Mum; do we have to?"   But as usual, when it came round to bed time, mum got her way. So after a long bubble bath, the boys retired to their bedroom, milk drink and biscuits in their hand.
It wasn't long before both boys were fast asleep in their beds.

Jenny, Silvia, and Fred were enjoying their supper, it had been a long day, and in forty eight hours it would be Christmas Eve
Fred was sitting by the window in the kitchen. "Did you see that; he put his cup down, "Now what do you suppose that was?" Silvia peered out into the night sky; and shaking her head. Said "No I didn't see anything; and turning to Jenny "did you Mum?" "Well I though I saw a shooting star and a peculiar shape flying up there,   but it couldn't be, it's too dark" Silvia turned to her Mum, "If we pulled the curtains on at night, we wouldn't see anything"

Further Secrets of the Garden

Silvia had tried for some time to get her Mum to draw the curtains at night; but Jenny had always said, there was no need, as they weren't over looked. The closest neighbours; were at the other end of the long drive; besides, from the kitchen window she could look out on Billy's Garden.

The shooting star in question was in fact the Gnome Beam. Keeper, who had been aware of everything that had gone on since the day Billy Potts had passed away, had noticed the special love the boy's had for the gnomes, they were doing their best to take care of the little chaps, and as far as he could see, they were making a pretty good job of it. This is why he had allowed extra time for the Gnome beam to retain power. Firstly; so he could catch Jake Wilmot, secondly, he knew what would happen when the flood came. The Gnomes would need the extra power to cope with that disaster.

But now tonight, he was on a different mission. He was going to take Archie and Joe Potts on a wonderful magic adventure. They deserved a treat; and what's more they were going to get one.

The light that Silvia had seen was in fact. Keeper, steering the Gnome beam into position, and the dark shape flying? Well that would soon be revealed to Archie and Joe Potts.

Archie and Joe tired after their night of building the castle had fallen asleep almost as soon as their heads hit the pillow.

Keeper had waited his time, he had been preparing this for a long time, and now the time had come. He had manoeuvred the Gnome beam carefully so that it shone on both boys at the same time. The soft spell, he had used before to put the boy's in a dreamlike state and Jenny in a trance back at the party, was a good spell, it was kind, and did no harm.

Joe was the first to move. Followed by Archie, a few moment's later. The Gnome beam, seemed to gather in strength, it enveloped both boy's. They were lifted from their beds, and into the Gnome beam. Strange thing was! They were still asleep and snuggled beneath the covers it was though they had been lifted out of themselves; although to all intents the boys were still in bed!

The boys began to glide upwards; they were both awake and smiling. Once they were
secure inside the beam, they left the bedroom, sailed through the window, and soon they were high in the sky. The Gnomebeam felt lovely and warm, the boys were enveloped in a pink glow. From somewhere above music was playing, Not the music Archie and Joe were used to, But both boys recognised the sweet haunting sound.
Up and up they went, until finally they came to a tunnel.

Joe was the first to speak. He glanced towards his brother. "Are you alright Arch?" The younger boy nodded his head. He reckoned he had never felt as happy as this, apart from when MOLAC and the other Gnomes had been found safe and sound.

Unbeknown to both boys Keeper had put a warm, safe spell on them otherwise the journey to YUMPLAND would have been very traumatic for them both.

He had decided that because they had shown great love for the gnomes, he would take them on the adventure of their lives. After all the Potts brothers were the first boys to have the job of caring for the Gnomes, for as far back as two hundred years, the job had been taken care of by grown ups. Algernon Potts being the first man to have any dealings with the Gnomes He had been the one to bring them back from Bavaria well over a hundred years ago. Algernon had bought them from the old Peasant who had made them. Algernon had been travelling through Bavaria, when he was struck down with a fever. The story was that

the Peasant took care of Algernon .and when he recovered
he stayed on in Bavaria, until the old Peasant died.

The old man had magic powers, and he had put the magic
into the Gnomes. The story went; that as long as they were
loved they would come to life every hundred years.
And of course, Keeper had always been in control.

The old Bavarian Peasant had recognised in Algernon
Potts this gift of love. So he had sold them to the fellow
knowing that his Gnomes would be loved and taken care
of. The Gnomes had carried on down the Potts line, until
they reached Billy Potts. All the carer's had been grown
ups until Archie and Joe Potts, hence the treat the Archie
and Joe were enjoying at the moment.

CHAPTER 13

YUMPLAND

The boys entered the tunnel, the haunting music became louder………Then they saw something they recognised from the garden party they had enjoyed last year before their Granddad had died. Coming towards them where two Beamins, these were the orb like creatures that had floated about the garden party, carrying little gold trays, on which they carried the magic food, one orb was a bright orange in colour the other purple.

Archie and Joe floated upwards together. The younger brother hadn't taken his eyes from the brightly coloured Beamins. "Is this real Joe, or are we dreaming?" Joe feeling gobsmacked, answered, "Don't know broth, but if I'm dreaming, I don't want to wake up" The boys would be in this dream like state for one night only. But many Magical adventures were going to happen during that time. It would seem to them rather timeless in content. But time wasn't an issue. To all intents and purposes the boys would be back in their beds and all would be as it was. Well nearly all!

The boys reached the end of the tunnel. They stopped moving forward, but they seemed to hang suspended in thin air. A door in front of them that looked to be made of marshmallow slowly opened. A soft brown voice spoke. "Come in Archie and Joe, you are very welcome"

The boys were looking at a man in a flowing white robe. A tall man, easily nine foot high, his hair was pure white falling over his shoulders and seemed to reach his middle back. He had a beard, also pure white in colour. His eyes were the kindest either boy had ever seen, the brightest blue. In his hand he carried a long pole.

He spoke again. "Welcome boys; I hope you will enjoy your time in YUMPLAND. We have much to show you, please follow me" With that the boys stepped through the marshmallow door.

Both boys looked in awe at what was before them. Firstly, instead of walking, they floated, holding on to each other for support. Keeper noticing the boy's difficulty;
"Don't worry boys; you will soon get used to the light feeling you are experiencing at the moment; we have very little gravity on YUMPLAND; we are a small planet; you will soon get used to the feeling; and use it to your advantage eventually"

It didn't take very long before Archie and Joe were doing summersaults; owing to their lightness of body. Keeper asked" Would you boys like some refreshment?"
Archie nodded, "Yes please" keeper put up his hand and hailed somebody away in the distance. Archie and Joe were overawed at the creature that came gliding towards them.

Archie said, in a hushed whisper;   "Look Joe, it's a man Gnome; he reminds me of MOLAC"   The Gnome man; smiled at the boys, "Come this way. They were shown to a building that resembled a large upturned flowerpot. It stood about as big as the workshop back home. It was bright yellow in colour, the domed roof was black the door was wide open. The Gnome man showed them inside.   There were a scattering of tables and chairs, all were different colours. They reminded Joe of the chairs and tables back at primary school. The walls were covered in pictures of smiling Gnomes, some looking very old and distinguished.

The little Gnome man bade them be seated. Archie being that bit smaller than Joe just managing with a wriggle, to get his knee's under the table. Joe sat sideways.
"What would you like to order," said the Gnome man. Archie smiled. The Gnome man did look like his favourite

Gnome. Joe piped up with "What have you got?" Well; said the gnome, "You can order anything you want; and it will be brought to the table" Joe addressed his brother, "What do you fancy Arch?" The boy glanced again at the MOLAC looking gnome. "I would like sausage and chips please" No sooner had the request been made, Than an Orb, of brilliant blue ,carrying a gold tray on which was a plate full of the requested food. It was placed on the table before Archie. The aroma coming from the plate of sausage and chips, was mouth wateringly good.

Now it was Joe's turn to order. His choice was a big beef burger and chips, no sooner had he said it than the chosen food appeared. The boys tucked into the meal and as they did, Joe almost choked on a mouthful of beef burger, at what happened next. His chair was facing the café door, he had just taken a bite of food, when an animal resembling a lion came walking towards him, followed by a hippopotamus. They were both smaller in size to the ones back home, but all the same they were wild animals. Archie, noticing his brother's demeanour, "What's up Joe" The elder boy was trying to signal with his eyes, when Archie turned round to be confronted with what had scared Joe.

The animals walked over to where the boys were, and to the amazement of both. The Lion sat down at Archie's feet and put his head on the lad's knee. The Hippopotamus had ambled over to the other side of the table, and was sitting down by Joe.
These two animals were much smaller than the ones back home, but all the same, both Archie and Joe were very scared. Just then, the MOLAC look alike came back and noticing the boys frightened appearance.

"Don't worry Archie and Joe; the animals will not harm you; let me introduce to them. The Gnome man walked over to the Hippopotamus. "This is LUMA and walking towards

Archie; he touched the Lion. Let me introduce you to BRAK"

Joe and Archie; were in a state of shock, neither boy daring to move a muscle; just sat and stared at the animals. The next thing to happen was so unbelievable, that if they hadn't been there, they wouldn't have believed it. BRAK; lifted his head from Archie's knee stretched towards the lad, and with a big blue tongue, proceeded to lick his face. Archie, gobsmacked; was taken aback. He was looking straight into the gentle eyes of the softest Lion. He put out his hand and touched the Lion's thick mane.
BRAK began to pure like a giant cat; the sound reverberating through Archie's body.
The lion's tongue was warm and damp, his breath sweet.
Archie looked across at Joe. This couldn't be happening it wasn't real. It was all a dream.

Joe meanwhile was being entertained by LUMA. She was sitting by the boy's side
He was gently stroking her giant back.   At one point the Hippopotamus opened her great mouth. But it was only to yawn.

Keeper suddenly appeared on the scene. "Ah' I see BRAK and LUMA have introduced themselves?"   He smiled, "Come on boys we have much to see"
With that, Archie and Joe left the table and followed Keeper out side. They tried to walk, but owing to the lack of gravity, the boys floated and glided. on their way. They were about to see, and be told the most magical sights and sounds they had ever seen.

They were taken down a winding path, on either side there were strange buildings.
They resembled large upturned flower pots in a variety of colours. One was very, very, large, and looked to be made of gold. It was almost as big as the workshop back home,

some small; .but none any smaller than a dustbin. All were beautifully painted.
It reminded the boys of the rainbow, they saw sometimes over the garden back home, after a summer storm.

All of a sudden, from out of the dwellings came a throng of strange little people, except they weren't really people.
They were all Gnomes; but moved like people' they spoke like people, but they were Gnomes?   Keeper called the Gnome people over to him.
"Come and meet Archie and Joe from the cottage in the' Big land 'beyond the Gnome Beam, They are the ones I told you about; The boys who take care of your honorary brother's back in their own land"

The Gnome like people gathered round Archie and Joe, and in voices similar to the one's they had heard in Granddad's workshop' The strange little people began to hum. As they did; the Gnome men, put their arms out to the side, and then reached up to the deep blue sky in unison; swaying back and forth, back and forth.. Archie remembered vividly MOLAC and the other Gnomes, doing the self same thing at the garden party before Granddad had died, said to his brother "What do you think of all this Joe, is it really happening?" Joe nodded. "It must be real we are both experiencing the same thing"   We both travelled up the Gnome Beam, and in a hushed voice, and what about the funny animals?"   Keeper interrupted the conversation between the boys.

"I have already explained the reason for your visit to YUMPLAND; It is a reward for all the kindness shown to our brother Gnomes back in your own land.; As I said earlier, you two boys are the only youngsters to be involved with caring for MOLAC, and his brother Gnomes, back in your land, and it is in recognition of that fact, that I thought it fitting to give you boys the thrill of your lives. After all; you are the very first, and probably the only ones to have ever been invited to enter our Gnome Beam or

YUMPLAND." Keeper; sounding rather serious, "and I must tell you; this visit is also part of the secret. "It must remain secret." Archie and Joe nodded to Keeper, besides, who would believe them? They didn't know anyone else who had glided up a Gnome Beam and been in the company of a lion and a Hippopotamus and what about the gnome people. No this was real alright, and it belonged only to them.

The MOLAC, Look alike came half walking half gliding towards the boys, and taking Archie by the hand. said in a rubble gruff sort of voice. "Come on, we have much to show you"
Archie was surprised. The little Gnome man felt warm to the touch. With his other hand he took hold of Joe. The elder brother felt a bit daft, fancy holding hands with a Gnome, and a warm one at that!

They were led down a path that ran by the side of a river. It looked like a river back home except the water was full of noise. It sounded like a lot of people all talking at once.
All of a sudden, a large bright blue fish put his head out of the water, wriggled a bit
and said in a quick gargle sort of voice "Hello you two, glad you came to visit" Archie and Joe stopped where they were. The Gnome who was holding their hands said, "The fish talk too much; they jabber all day. They never stop"
Archie spoke now. "What do you mean; Fish can't talk?"
The Gnome man smiled, "Well you heard that one didn't you?, they do here" Sometimes the water is bubbling with their voices, especially when they are all talking at once, the blue fish being the noisiest"

"Are there different coloured fish then?" The Gnome man looked at Joe. "Oh yes Joe; all the colours of the rainbow" The pink and white ones are the quietest, we don't see those very much, rather shy, they are rather bullied by the noisier blue ones."

Archie thought for a moment. That seemed a little unfair. "Well what about fish and chips then?" I bet you don't have those, how can you eat talking fish"

The Gnome man answered. "No we don't eat talking fish. In fact we don't east fish at all in YUMPLAND. Mind you, this is the only place where you will find talking fish. None of the other galaxies have them, not talking ones anyway" "So like you down on your planet they probably do eat them with chips, but as for us; no, we don't eat our friends, and I say friend loosely, sometimes the blue ones drive us mad, but we still couldn't eat them" Archie and Joe were pleased with that. It didn't seem right to eat something you could have a conversation with. This was a strange place and no mistake, and it was about to become stranger.

They were taken next into a cave by the Gnome man. "Now don't be frightened you are about to meet the resident of the cave" Their eyes soon became accustomed to the dark. As they moved forward the boys could make out a large cavern. It was enormous, on the walls were what appeared to be lights small green blue red and purple in colour, which seemed to have just come on as they entered, and seemed to be humming! The cavern was now like a fairy land. In the background they could hear a strange noise, a large billowing sound. Was it somebody or something breathing?" The big noise was scary. Joe, who was supposed to be the brave one, grabbed tight hold of Archie's arm, "Don't go any further Broth we don't know what's in the cave?" Archie stood where he was, shook his head, and in a quiet voice said. "No I won't Joe. I don't like the sound of that either"

Well they were about to find out just what had made the strange noises, and what they saw and heard next was almost beyond belief. From the back of the cave, the noise of breathing and snorting became almost deafening. The first thing to come into view was a long plume of fire. Both boys stepped back in alarm. Archie opened his mouth to yell, but nothing came out.

Further Secrets of the Garden

Coming lumbering towards them was the largest Dragon you could ever imagine. To Joe's reckoning he must have been as tall as the cottage back home.

The Dragon stopped in front of them and to the utter amazement of the terrified brothers, he opened his enormous mouth and out came a booming but sugar coated voice.

"Well, hello there boys, my name is Volt, glad to meet you both at last, don't be scared of me. I am a big softy. Dragons are supposed to be fearsome I know, but not me. My goodness, I sometimes scare myself I am so big and noisy, and the flames! Well they are a bit over the top. But I suppose Dragons must have flames, its tradition you know, although I believe I am the last Dragon of all" with that the Dragon sighed noisily. As he did so a puff of smoke came down his nose.

Archie and Joe were looking up into the daftest face they had ever seen on a Dragon. He had the softest big green eyes, the biggest set of teeth and the longest purple tongue that he kept flicking in and out. The boys kept their eyes firmly on the enormous beast making sure to duck as the blue tongue came within licking distance. The Dragon sent another plume of fire above their heads. Archie and Joe ducked once more. This was very scary. The dragon looked friendly. But because neither had ever met such a monster as this before it was best to be careful, they didn't fancy being Dragon food.   The Dragon threw out yet another plume of fire and coughed loudly said to the startled pair. "I wish I could stop doing that, it makes my throat sore; but it's what Dragons do you know"

The Gnome man looked up at the Dragon. "Hello Volt; and how are you today?"

The Dragon, looked down on the gnome man, and craning his long neck towards,
him shook his giant head, at the same time blowing out of his mouth a whiff of smoke, with a hint of flame. He

answered with a slight cough in his throat the enquiring little Gnome.

"As you see me Lubon as you see me" You will notice that I am still having trouble with the flames, just can't stop blowing them out, my throat is driving me nuts?"
With that the giant Dragon, looked towards Joe and Archie. The boys in absolute amazement stared back. Well they had never seen a real Dragon before they had read stories in books and seen them on film- but never in real life! The Dragon's face came close. . Joe stepped back, but Archie was rooted to the spot. Volt opened his great mouth. Archie was closer to a set of enormous blackened teeth than he cared to be.

The Dragon cocked his horned head to one side and in a surprisingly soft voice said,. "I have waited a long time to meet you two" Just then a thin plume of fire whistled past Archie's ear. Volt gave a cough, "Oh there I go again; this is getting beyond a joke; don't be scared; I do so hate doing that every time I open my mouth; its such bad manners"

Archie put his hand to the side of his head and ear and then looked at it for any signs of burnt hair. "It's alright Dragon you didn't burn me" The Dragon gave a big sigh.
"Well that's a relief Archie, and you needn't keep calling me Dragon! We know each other now; my name is Volt; call me Volt, and by the way, don't keep calling the YUMPOIDS GNOME MEN, You will hurt their feelings"
Archie and Joe nodded to the giant of a creature. They were glad to know what the little men were called. But they couldn't really be blamed for refereeing to them as Gnomes' they so resembled MOLAC and the rest of the Gnomes back home. Archie, with a pain in his neck from looking up reckoned he was in the presence of the tallest Dragon he had ever seen in his entire life.

But the boy wondered how the Dragon could possibly say he knew them? Neither he nor Joe had ever seen Volt before.

Joe addressed Volt. "When you say you have been waiting to meet us for a long time, what exactly do you mean?" The Dragon raised himself up to his full height, which was pretty huge. He then sat down with a bump that seemed to shake the cave. As he did this, his enormous tail stretched out behind him and flicked up into the top of the cave the boys looked in utter amazement at this great tail. It appeared to be very thick at the bottom of his back it seemed to narrow until finally it tapered off to a thin coil. On the very end was an appendage, resembling a fat spear. He had horns on his head and down his back. He also had scaly wings which he shook vigorously two or three times as he settled himself down. His body was a dark greeny brown in colour which appeared to change at times to almost black, and his eyes; they were of a yellow colour with flecks of pink and orange, they were so gentle to look at, set in a very funny face. Well, funny for a Dragon that is!

It was Archie and Joe's turn to cough and splutter as bits of scale and dead skin cascaded from the dragon's wings and almost covered them.

Volt, seeing the mess he had caused. Said, "I'm sorry boys, but its moulting season for Dragons. Mind you I'm the only Dragon left; but this seems to happen every time the sun turns over and every thing gets hotter; The Yumpoid's don't care for it either, brings them out in big purple spots. They don't moult though; not like me"

Archie and Joe began to brush themselves down, some of the Dragon scales were rather hard to get rid of they seemed to stick to their pyjamas. The Dragon, with a soppy look on his face said "Let me help you. Boys" He

pursed his lips to blow. Archie remembered the flames. "No Volt; please don't blow" But it was too late.
The Dragon took in a deep breath and blew, luckily for the boys the flame left the dragon's mouth and sailed over their heads. Volt gave a gasp. "Oh I've just got to stop doing that it's ridiculous; my throat won't stand much more"

Archie and Joe looked up at the trouble Dragon. Archie spoke. "Do you have honey and ice cream on Yumpland?" The Dragon nodded. "Yes we do: but what do either have to do with my sore throat?" The Yumplanders make a sort of delicious sweet with the honey; very sticky,; and the ice cream; well, that is eaten by the Yumplanders only on special occasions like Yumpland Day and Big Moon Night At these times lots of Ice cream is eaten by the Yumpoid's along with sweet Honey Brew., they seem to love this" makes them very happy. Trouble is when they are preparing this Brew, you can smell it all over Yumpland, to tell the truth, the smell has had me tail down and half asleep more than once"

The boys listened to what the Dragon had to say. They thought they had a solution to the sore throat problem; the fire throwing episodes would need to be thought about very carefully.
"Have you ever had honey to soothe your throat" Asked Joe." Mum always gives us a spoonful when we have a sore throat" Archie piped up next; not wanting to be left out of giving the good advice. "And Ice cream; she gives us ice cream as well"

Volt looked at both boys in alarm. "YUK! and, again; YUK! Honey and ice cream for a Dragon's throat!! Who ever heard of such a sticky thing? I don't think so" With that the Dragon began to turn himself round, and with a shake and a swish of his giant wings Volt began to amble towards the front of the cave, and prepared to fly away.

Archie raised himself up. "But Volt- Please don't leave; Honey is well known in our land for soothing sore throats, and ice cream cools the area"

The giant Dragon, not heading the plea to stay extended and flapped his wings, and leaving a thunderous sounding wind behind him Volt flew up into the sky and as if in defiance a large plume of fire shot up into space from his mouth- The Dragon was heard to cough and splutter very loudly.

Joe and Archie were upset at the Dragon's attitude. "Archie turned to his brother, "Do you think we will ever see Volt again?" Joe answered. "Don't know Broth, just don't know; can't think what upset him?"

Just then Lubon, the Yumpoid came into the cave, the boys knew his name now since Volt had addressed him earlier, and they also knew the true name of the Gnome men, they wouldn't be making the same mistake again, although Archie had to admit he thought Yumpoid's a funny name, for something that looked so like a Gnome. "Don't concern yourselves too much about the state of the Dragon's throat said Lubon, he worries about the state of it so much and he probably thought your talk of honey and ice cream for his condition, rather foolish, to tell the truth it's a new one on me"

Archie asked. "But why did Volt fly away, we only wanted to help him?" Ludon shook his head. "Don't worry too much; he will be back, perhaps you could tell me all about how honey and Ice cream help you; for we have never known of any such thing; We make a special drink from the Honey; on two occasions only; they are Big Moon Night and Yumpland Day. The drink is very much appreciated by all the Yumplanders. It is very sweet you know; makes everyone jolly; and the ice cream,
This also is a treat, only to be eaten on these two occasions" Lubon paused for breath.

"Now Archie and Joe, perhaps you can tell me about how these two special treats can possibly help Volt and his sore throat; for such a thing seems impossible to me, but please tell me anyway"

Joe began first. "Well it's a well known thing in our house; Mum always gives us a big spoonful of honey at the first sign of a cold or sore throat" Lubon interrupted, " I know about a sore throat, because of Volt suffering with one; But what is a cold?"
Joe looked at his brother, Archie piped up with" Well that can be a sore throat, and it makes you sneeze as well; and you have to keep blowing your nose cos the cold makes it run." Lubon asked "What is run, blowing nose and sneeze; I don't know these things?"

Archie and Joe looked at each other how were they possibly going to explain this to Lubon, when the Gnome man had never heard of a common cold.

Archie began. "Well it's like this Lubon. Down on our planet we have illnesses called a cold, sometimes we have other illnesses much worse than a cold, these can make you very ill, he was recalling the time Joe went into hospital with appendicitis. His mum had told him all about it, she had said the big word. He remembered Joe being very sick. And his Gran had suffered a bad leg some time ago, and their mum had quite a few headaches. Archie often wondered what a headache was.

The boys did their best to explain, about being ill on their planet, how honey and ice cream helped when they had a cold, honey to soothe the sore throat and ice cream to cool it down. Archie added that the ice cream was definitely the best part of the getting better. But they could tell the Yumpoid didn't really understand, he kept telling them about what happened in Yumpland and it was very different to what they were used to down on earth, in fact It sounded very good.

Apparently, Yumpoid's never got sick. Lubon explained that at a given time, after many years of living in Yumpland, a light would appear behind the left ear of the Yumpoid who's time it was, and when that happened, the Yumpoid simply was no more. This light in turn transferred to the wall in the cave, where it shown forever in all the colours of the big bow of light that comes over Yumpland after a shower. Joe said, Yes I know it. "It's what we call a rainbow, we have it as well" Lubon smiled and carried on. "Volt is in charge of the caves and the Yumplights. He is responsible for making sure they shine correctly, charge them up now and again, some of the Yumpoid's have been shining in the cave for hundreds of years. The lights hum and sing you know, every time a new Yumpoid joins them, it is an enchanted place, very much revered by all us living in Yumpland. We all like to spend time there it's a good place we especially enjoy the time you refer to as GNOME BEAM NIGHT" Lubon had surprised the boys with this statement.

"I think both you boys will know what I meant when I said Gnome beam night" Archie and Joe looked at Lubon, they were both shocked. But thinking about it, Archie said to his brother. "Why should we be so surprised, after all wasn't it Keeper who sent the so called Gnome Beam down on that special night last year before Granddad died?" Joe nodded. This adventure was becoming more fantastic by the minute. Lubon interrupted the boys. Ah yes, last year. That sure was very special. We worked hard to make sure the party went with a swing. You deserved it; for carrying on the tradition of loving our Honorary Gnome brothers.

Archie and Joe stood open mouthed.
"You mean to say that MOLAC and the rest of the Gnomes who live in our garden are actually related to you; said Archie?" Lubon appeared to think for a moment. "Well not related like you and your brother. I don't know if you are aware of the story; but MOLAC and his brothers were made in the northern end of your planet by an old Bavarian

peasant many years ago. An old travelling ancestor of yours brought them back to your part of the galaxy when the old peasant died they were passed down the family line until they came to you two, and because it was obvious you loved them and it had come round to the hundred year celebration we introduced some special magic of our own"

If Archie and Joe had been puzzled before; they sure were now. "But if what you say
is true about an old Bavarian Peasant making our Gnomes. Who made the YUMPOIDS and how can they possibly be anything to do with MOLAC, LAGREN' and the rest of our Gnomes?"

Lubon took a deep breath. "Well Archie and Joe. I will do my best to explain. We Yumplanders have been here for many years; long before your Gnomes were made. Archie piped up, "More than a hundred?" Lubon smiled, "More than two thousand years Archie; Volt has been here longer than that. We have always been Gnome like; as you put it; so when, a couple of hundred years ago Gnome figures were being made down on your planet, that so resembled us Yumpoid's, We began to take an interest. Keeper was especially intrigued, and sort of adopted them as our brothers, we have kept our eyes on them ever since; it was Keeper who gave them the power of speech and eventual movement; and it is him to thank for your involvement with MOLAC and the rest. In fact it is all due to Keepers magic. "Your Gnomes are so like us you see we couldn't help but love them, and you also love the Gnomes that is very obvious, and that is why you are both here, as a thank you .Your Gnomes have been our Gnomes so to speak ever since they were first cut from rock and fashioned in our image many years ago. Keeper took it as a sign that they were somehow linked to us, and therefore belonged to us in a small way"   Lubon stopped and looked around..

"That reminds me; it's about time the Dragon was back in the cave; he belongs to us also, we take care of our own. Perhaps you can explain to the silly big lump that you only wanted to help him when you suggested honey and ice cream for his sore throat. He'd never heard of it you see, he thought you were making fun of him, he's rather temperamental for a Dragon. Mind you, as I said before honey and ice cream for a sore throat that's a new one on me"

Archie and Joe were fascinated by what Lubon had said about the Yumplanders being
here long before the Gnomes back home. Joe asked Lubon if MOLAC and the rest of their Gnomes knew about the Yumpoid's and life on Yumpland.

Lubon thought for a moment. "Well they understand in part that there is a stronger power that comes from above. Only in part; for to know the full extent of our involvement in their welfare; would be too much for them to cope with.
Suffice to say they know enough about a stronger being taking care of their welfare,
They know about Gnome Beam Night, they understand the music that flows down the Beam on special occasions. They know and revere Keeper; they understand he gave them the power of speech and feelings; apart from that, the answer to your question is no, it would be far too much knowledge for them to take in"

Joe asked. "What about Volt, do they know about him?" Lubon shook his head. ."No
your Gnomes know nothing of the Dragon, He is aware of them though, it was Volt who went down to your planet with Keeper on the night they were stolen by the builder; and it was Volt who got into the mind of the thief when he was stopped in his tracks with the box of stolen gnomes by the power of the Beam. Lubon smiled.
"It will be a long time, before the builder tries that trick again. Volt scared the man almost out of his pants. And

talking about Volt..   It's about time he came back from wherever he's gone, If he doesn't come soon I will have to go looking for him, he can be so tiresome at times"

Archie and Joe asked if they could accompany Lubon in the search "After all" said Archie, it was us who upset Volt with the talk of Honey and ice cream for his sore throat." Lubon looked at the boys, "Alright then, we may as well start looking now but don't be surprised if he ignores you; he can be such a wimp"   With that, the three set off in search of the Dragon.

CHAPTER 14

AN UNBELIEVABLE ADVENTURE

The boys followed Lubon from the cave. This time they were going in quite a different direction to the one that had brought them to the cave. They crossed a sturdy bridge that straddled the river where all the talking fish lived. The blue ones were as usual gabbling together and on seeing Lubon. "VOLT WENT THAT WAY" the fish shouted loudly. Towards the big hill where he spends most of his time" The blue fish were clamouring towards the other side of the river the water seemed to be boiling and bubbling so fierce was their leaping up and talking at the same time, was absolutely deafening.

"STOP YOU FISH, BE QUIET I SAY"   Lubon had shouted so loudly, that the noise brought Joe and Archie to a stand still.   The equally noisy blue fish on hearing Lubon's deafening roar quietened down. The timid white and pink fish, who didn't like to be loud, thanked the Yumpoid for his intervention. Lubon nodded his head to the little fish, .he felt sorry for them.

Archie removed his hands from his ears.   "Why are the blue fish so noisy Lubon"   The Yumpoid shook his head, "Don't know Archie, they have always been the same?" Mind you, there may be a very good reason. It seems that years ago, when Yumpland was a young planet the fish and the Dragon's were the only inhabitants. I say Dragon's, because there were two in the beginning. Archie and Joe listened with interest.   Joe spoke up. "Do you mean Volt had a partner Lubon?" Can't say for sure Joe; but Volt talks of the other Dragon eating the blue fish, if she could catch them that is" Apparently the fish used to be quiet. That was until the female Dragon came on the scene with her sharp teeth, purple piercing eyes, and an appetite for blue fish. They developed a voice over many years, sort of a warning system to each other when the female Dragon was on the

hunt for a meal. The thing is boys; Volt doesn't like fish as a food" He would never think of these blue annoyances as a tasty meal; rather an aggravation, I think it bothered Volt that his partner had such a cruel streak.
He's a big softie you see, and may I say a trifle touchy. As you boy's already know"

"What happened to the female Dragon Lubon" Joe was really getting into this whole affair and wanted to know all the details. Lubon answered the boy rather wistfully.

"Well according to Volt; his partner finished up very badly and it apparently hit Volt
hard, and it took him a long time to get over the trauma. It seems the female Dragon choked on a large blue fish bone; and fell down dead at his feet. Of course, this was long before us Yumpoid's came on the scene. But if you want to see where the female Dragon finished up I am sure Volt will show you, that is when we find him, and when he gets over his sulk. He spends a good part of his time just sitting at the place where he laid her to rest. He's a funny old thing really, couldn't get on with her when she was alive, yet he sits for hours by the place where he put her in the ground, and I think if I'm not mistaken that is where we will find Volt now"

This was very interesting to both boys. What an adventure they were having. Nobody would ever believe this. Well Gran would when they told her. So would MOLAC and the other Gomes. But nobody else must know the secret. They couldn't tell anyone else. No! This was too special.   They could hardly believe this was real themselves, but it was, every bit of it- they knew it was completely real.

"Come on boys follow me, and keep close to me , we need to go through the forest of upside down trees, and exploding bright red mushrooms, be very careful not to step on these mushrooms; they make a terrible mess of your boots, and if you're not careful they grab at your ankles" Archie piped up. "We are not wearing boots Lubon, only our slippers and pyjamas"

"Well" said Lubon. "You will need to be extra careful then, the thing is the mushrooms are very wary at this time of year. It is almost harvest time, the Yumpoid gatherers harvest as many as they can; the mushrooms on the other hand do their best to stop themselves from being gathered, that is why they grab at your ankles. You see boy's if they can be collected before they explode they make a tasty snack. If not, then it's too late and the harvest is lost for another year, and we have a terrible mess to clean up"

Joe and Archie listened to what Lubon was saying. "Are the mushrooms alive then?"
And what do you mean when you say they maker a mess?" Joe was very interested in this, he liked a bit of gore. Lubon smiled, "Well, in a way I suppose they are alive, but not as we are living and breathing; and the mess well' that needs to be seen to be believed"

Archie asked what Lubon meant. "Well boy, it isn't very nice, when it comes round to Gathering time, the mushrooms do their best to stop the gatherers; they have a sticky mechanism which; when touched releases the explosion of health giving nutrients that us Yumpoid's need, the goodness is lost, we have a terrible mess of sticky muck to clean up, this is why you must be careful when we go through the forest, the mushrooms know the time is almost here for the Yumpoid gatherer's to start work. So you must be careful not to step on them,. if you do, they will grab hold of your boots, in your case slippers, you will be covered in sticky red sludge that will take ages to get rid of, and they won't let go, I remember some years ago, a Yumpoid gatherer, got so stuck it took about ten of us brothers to free him; he had to give up his gathering after that. He said he couldn't get over the fear he had felt being grabbed at, and held by the horrible slimy mushrooms. He helps Volt now to take care of the lights in the cave. Mind you, when we are able to harvest the goodness from the mushrooms; it is put into giant tanks and stored. The taste, when collected at the right time; is absolutely divine and very precious to us Yumpoid's" Lubon stopped talking. "Now come on boy's, that's enough about mushrooms, we must find Volt"

The three entered the forest of upside down trees, Archie and Joe looked around. This was like no forest they had ever seen. Back home there was a wood nearby, a nice wood, almost a forest where they sometimes went for a walk with the family. Their Gran especially enjoyed the stroll through the lovely area. But it was a recognisable wood, but this place was nothing like anything the boys had experienced before.

The trees were definitely upside down, thick roots sticking up in the air like grotesque figures, spider like in appearance. The sky above the upside down forest looked odd also, very dark blue in colour, the boy's had never seen such a strong vibrant blue, not back home anyway. Still they weren't at home now, they were in Yumpland so anything could happen.

Lubon and the boys pressed on through the forest of weird looking trees, being very careful as they went. When all of a sudden, just in front of them came a peculiar sounding voice. "Hi there Lubon; my oh my; remember what you told Archie and Joe "MIND THE EXPLODING MUSHROOMS" Well' you almost stepped on one yourself Lubon; and again came the friendly rebuke; "My oh my; that will never do"

Lubon looked to where the voice was coming from. "Oh hello there Spik, I thought it might be you, how are things?" Spik nodded to the Yumpoid and looked beyond Lubon to the boys. Archie and Joe thought they had seen and heard everything. But here in front of them was the biggest and most colourful bird they had ever seen. He stood about as big as Farmer Lambert's prize bull. His body was bright pink, his wings buttercup yellow. His big feet and skinny legs were bright orange, and he could talk!!

Spik opened his pure white beak again, and with green eyes that spoke of kindness he addressed Archie and Joe. "It's nice to meet you two at last. Did you enjoy the journey? ,it's quite a long way you know" The big bird preened and stretched.." What do you think of Yumpland so far? Do you realise that you are the only children to visit us ever?" Archie and Joe were too awe-struck by this colourful talking bird to utter a single word. They just stood mesmerised by what they were witnessing. Spik continued to speak. ."We all knew you were going to pay us a visit; we are miles away from your own planet you know; you have travelled a great distance to get here,
and may I say that you are very welcome" and as an after thought Spik spoke to the boys with a broad smile around his beak.
"Pity you are not colourful like us, we love colour you know" and once again the big bird preened himself. He turned to Lubon once more.
"What brings you this way; are you looking for Volt again?" Lubon nodded. "What's upset the Dragon this time Lubon? I expect the big lump will be in his usual place; I can't understand Volt needing to spend so much time just sitting by that big sad hill after all this time, can you?" Spik fluttered his buttercup yellow wings, at the same time stretching his fat neck upwards and shaking his head he waited for an answer.

Lubon gave a sigh. He secretly thought to himself that Spik was a very vain bird. He could never say anything though, No that would never do. For all his faults, Spik was
a good friend, always helping out when the blue fish got out of control; and that was
quite often. They were so noisy; and always had been besides being a menace to the quieter pink and white fish. It seemed that when it came to controlling the terrible bullying blue fish; Spik came into his own. He couldn't

stand their racket either. But with a few well chosen words of command spoken loudly 'QUIET YOU FISH,' a low swoop, and a shake of his buttercup wings over the seething mass. Spik soon had the noisy blue creatures under control every time.

Lubon was glad of that, he couldn't work out why the bird had such control over the blue fish, but he was thankful anyway. Spik had actually informed him how to get the fish to conform when he wasn't in the vicinity. Lubon had found the words of command Spik had taught him very useful especially if he wore his yellow jacket. But what he didn't know, was that the buttercup wings had special power. The blue fish didn't like the colour yellow it sent them to sleep; and if they went to sleep for too long they would drown. Spik thought he may tell Lubon the secret one day, but it wouldn't hurt to keep quiet a little longer. Who knows he may impart the secret to Archie and Joe first.

Lubon addressed Spik. "Have you set your eyes on the Dragon; has he come this way?" Spik smiled and once again stretched his neck and shook his wings.
"Well I haven't actually seen him; but I felt the ground outside my borough shake this morning" Lubon nodded. "It sounds as though he came this way then, so we are on the right track" Archie interrupted the talk, And addressing the big bird once more. "What do you mean; your borough, don't you have a nest?" Spik turned his big body towards Archie, and looking down on the boy. "Nest' I don't have a nest; I'm much too big for a nest, my home is a big hole in the bank right inside the upside down forest" Archie pondered on this answer.
"Well how do you keep so clean then?" Spik puffed out his chest and smiling once more said." I preen my beautiful feathers boy; I preen every single day" Spik once more stretched his neck and opened his lovely white beak. . "That is how I stay so lovely"

Archie, intrigued now about this big bird having a home in the ground, asked Spik
"Can we see it then?" The bird looked towards Lubon and asked. "Do you have time to visit my home; or would you rather find Volt first?"

Lubon feeling rather anxious about the lost Dragon, said to Spik; "How about we pay you a call when we find the daft Dragon; I'm a little concerned about him?"
Spik bent his fat neck forward nodded his head and flapped his yellow wings once more. "Ok then boys; go with Lubon; find the Dragon and call on the way back and I will be happy to give you a tour of my home" With that, the big bird once again stretched his wings, fluttered loudly causing a mighty draught, turned his head towards the dark blue sky and with a leap, he took off, souring upwards. "See you later" he shouted, and as his voice became more and more distant; the three just managed to make out the words from the bird   "I promised LUMA a visit today"… Spik disappeared from view.

Lubon and the boys waved goodbye to Spik. "Give our love to the Hippopotamus" Said Lubon. See you when we come back"
Joe, intrigued more and more with events taking place, asked Lubon. "Do you mean to say that Spik and the Hippopotamus know each other?" Lubon smiled at the boy. "Why yes Joe; I told you before, we are all friendly in Yumpland, the only issues are those noisy blue fish, and Volt's moods, but we manage to keep them under control. I suppose even here in this beautiful place there are a few of issues to stop it being perfect, even the ankle grabbing mushrooms must be included in that statement"

Archie and Joe listened with interest to all Lubon had to say, they thought Yumpland a fascinating place. They were enjoying the visit; and didn't really want it to end. They realised it would come to a finish at some point. But they hoped not yet.

The three walked along slowly. Lubon knew this part of the Upside Down Forest; they had passed safely through the part where the exploding mushrooms were; and had arrived at an area equally important. Now they would be experiencing another special place.

Lubon explained to the boys that 'YANTRON' That was the name of this place; was very significant in the lives of the Yumpoid's. "If this place wasn't here- then neither would we"

Archie and Joe; intrigued that yet another place of importance was being discovered could hardly contain their curiosity. They moved slowly on, taking on board everything around them. Nothing was like anything they had ever seen before.

They came to the largest set of doors they had ever seen in their lives. "Wait here boys" Said a very important sounding Lubon "While I go and find Keeper, this is where our leader spends most of his time"

 The boys sat down on what looked like a large shiny stool to wait for Lubon, and looked around them at all the different points of interest. This sure was a place. They hadn't been seated for more than as second, when a voice from below their legs shouted.

"Excuse me; you are rather heavy on my shell" The boys startled, glanced down to where the voice was coming from. Archie spoke first to the creature that resembled a turtle. But this one had two heads each with a mouth full of teeth instead of a beak. "Sorry, but we thought you were a large stool" Archie looked at his brother. This was ridiculous; he was actually talking to a turtle with two heads!!   Joe, who hadn't moved a muscle, fell to the floor as the creature moved. Lubon was still within earshot of the boys and shouted back.

 "Don't worry about Trug, he won't hurt you, I should have warned you about him, he loves to sit there, he's a bit nosy; likes to see who's going in or out; but the old lad is harmless. Lubon, making sure Archie and Joe were alright, said "Won't be long boys, see you in a little while"

Trug spoke once more. This time; the voice came from the right hand mouth. The other he kept tightly shut, he only had one eye on each head; this was situated above the mouth of both scaly head's.

. "What do you think about Lubon?" Keeper relies on him he's very knowledgeable you know, oh yes he knows a lot" and with another smile from the head that was awake. "Will you be staying long in our land, or was this just a flying visit?" With that remark Trug showed his teeth and smiled with the mouth from one head only. The other head appeared to be sleeping still. The turtle noticing the boy's apparent disbelief in what they were witnessing. Smiled again and said drowsily.
"The past few hundred years I have begun to feel my age; so I only speak with one mouth at a time, resting the other for a while. Besides, I remember when I had both voices on the go at the same time; they used to chat all day long, very tiring you know; I can't stand it now, all I want is peace and quiet, any way boys, it looks like Lubon has found our leader, so I will say goodbye for now"

Archie and Joe were absolutely amazed at what they were experiencing; the situation just kept getting more and more bizarre, nobody in the world would ever believe this strange adventure, nobody. The boys left Trug and walked towards Lubon and Keeper. The big man with the gentle eyes, long grey hair and sweeping beard addressed Archie and Joe. The boys gazed up into the face of this gentle giant of a man. Keeper spoke.
"Now Archie and Joe Potts ; you have entered the heart beat of Yumpland; What you are about to experience in Yantron ; is something more wonderful than you have seen so far, try to prepare yourselves to be amazed at what you are about to be part of"

Stay close to Lubon, and he will explain what you are about to see" After a few more words with the Yumpoid, Keeper went ahead of them, and back into Yantron.

Lubon gestured to the boys to follow him, and pointed to a huge clock like mechanism; .which to Joe's reckoning (Him being the eldest, so he should know a bit more) must stand as tall as the church in the village back home but much-much wider. From what seemed to be the inside of the 'clock' there was the noise of a heavy whirring sound. As the boys watched intrigued at the sight before them, The hands on the clock face began to move, and at the same time laser like beams in brilliant colour seemed to spray out from the top in the direction of the building they were about to enter, beautiful colours of the rainbow showered high above the boys and cascaded towards another large object at the far end of the space. Joe, gob smacked by what he was witnessing, said to Archie, "Look at that broth; it's better than any fireworks I've ever seen in my life" Archie at this point was unable to speak.

Lubon, in a hushed voice, spoke to the boys. "Now Archie and Joe you are going to see something that you have never seen before; nor are you likely to see ever again, but I think in part you will understand better the things you have both experienced since being involved with your Gnomes back in your own land."

The boys in hushed silence followed Lubon towards Yantron As they got closer to the giant building; a mighty set of doors began to swing open, and at the same time beautiful music could be heard coming from inside. Archie held his breath. It was the same music that had come down the Gnome Beam at the first Gnome Beam Night Party when his Granddad was still alive, all those months ago.

Archie turned to his brother, and judging by the look on his face; Joe was recalling the self same memory. The eldest brother absolutely awe-struck, stood a bit closer to Archie as if to give himself courage. The giant doors finally came to a stop to reveal inside the most wonderful sight either boy had ever seen. Lubon taking in the magnitude of wonder on the faces of the boys; urged them inside the massive building. Both boys were completely taken aback at what came next. They were standing in a massive cathedral like building, with a ceiling that seemed to go on forever, higher and higher. The boys had to crane their necks to see the top. At the far end of the giant structure was what appeared to be a huge organ; again Joe estimated to be as big as the cottage back home. All of a sudden without warning the giant contraption seemed to come to life. Lubon gestured to the boys to cover their ears.

The coloured laser lights that had sprung from the massive clock earlier, were now dancing about on the organ keys. The boys recognised once again the beautiful music that had come down the Gnome beam at their garden party back home all those months ago.

Joe was just about to take a step towards the sound when Lubon took hold of his arm.

"No Joe don't go any further, just stand quite still and experience what happens next"

Both boys did as the Yumpoid asked, and watched with eyes wide open.

As the music from the mighty organ reached its crescendo, and more and more coloured laser lights cascaded onto what could only be described by the boy as the giant music machine. Then spears of light transferred to the floor in front of them. They in turn began to train on the centre of what looked to the boys like polished wood.

As the shards of coloured light focused on the centre of the floor- sections of wood began to separate into what could only be described as leaf shaped pieces. The music continued to play in the same haunting way. Slowly the opening became larger and larger. Archie and Joe hadn't moved at all since the floor had started to open.

Eventually, after what seemed like ages, the leaf shaped pieces of polished wood came to a stop and appeared disappear to reveal what looked to the boys to be a large stretch of water deep in a giant cavern, reached by a flight of steps that had been exposed as the floor disappeared.

Archie addressed Lubon." Is that a pond?" The Yumpoid, with a strange look on his face answered the boy.
"Well boy-I suppose you could call it that; but it is like no pond you two have ever seen"   The boys, peered down on the sight before them, it was beautiful. The water was contained in what looked like a large circular bath. Around the edge was a deep golden lip. In front of them was a set of steps leading down to the 'pond'

Lubon made a move forward. "Now boys, keep close to me and be careful as you go down, you are about to witness something most extraordinary-Well most strange to you two anyway "

Archie and Joe followed the Yumpoid down the steep steps. As they traversed downwards, Keeper appeared at the bottom. He was looking into the pool. Joe and Archie reached the bottom step. Keeper beckoned to them.
"Are you ready to be amazed boys?" Joe and his brother, without a word nodded to this gentle giant of a being.

Keeper beckoned both boys to stand by his side. Lubon looked on. "Now you are going to see something that will astound you a knowledge that will bring an understanding into why we know so much about you and your lives. Keeper looked down at his Guests." I don't think you realise just how much we in Yumpland owe to you?" Archie feeling a bit scared took hold of Joe's hand, it wasn't something he would normally do, but he was a bit frightened.

Joe feeling quite bewildered looked up at Keeper. The nine foot giant gestured to the boys to watch what happened next. They were standing in front this circular pool. Keeper raised his long staff and placed the tip into the centre of the water.

All of a sudden the surface of the water began to bubble and froth. The boys took a hasty step back. Lubon beckoned them forward once more. In a few moments the water turned a brilliant blue and settled down once more.

Keeper; leaning over the side of the blue water; stretched his arm towards the boys. Archie was the first to move and looked into the blue pool. He asked,
"Do you see anything boy?"   Archie feeling very scared now couldn't think what was supposed he looking for…but in a while his eyes became accustomed to the images in the water. He spoke in a hushed voice to his brother.
"It's our house; Look Joe it's our house can you see it's where we live?" This time Archie yelled out loudly." Look our Joe its MOLAC; and the rest of the Gnomes in Granddads workshop" Archie turned to Keeper. "But this is magic, how can you do this?" The boys continued to stare into the blue water. There came another image, this time it was Granddads garden at night, covered in snow.

Archie overcome with emotion at seeing his pal, waved frantically at MOLAC and at the same time calling out the Gnomes name.   Keeper spoke gently to Archie.
"There is no point calling and waving boy, the Gnome called, MOLAC; or in fact any of the other Gnomes, cannot see or hear you"

Keeper put a comforting arm around the boy's shoulder. This adventure was a lot for the boys to take in. He would try to explain further, why they had been chosen to experience this wonderful voyage of discovery. Keeper realised that no other boys past present or indeed in the foreseeable future would ever enjoy a similar adventure. It was definitely a one off.

The brothers carried on looking into the blue water. Granddads workshop looked the same, the garden looked the same; although it wasn't easy seeing it through the snow
that covered everything, and the Gnomes, they looked exactly as the boys remembered them. ABLEG and one of the lesser gnomes were still in need of being mended. Joe made a mental note. That would be the first job when they got back home.   Joe took a deep breath. Back home seamed a long way away. What an adventure they were having, and unbeknown to the boys, it was to continue for quite a time yet.

CHAPTER 15

VOLT AND THE THANKYOU RIDE

Keeper spoke to the Yumpoid. "Now Lubon, I suppose you had better go and bring that silly Dragon back from his usual haunt, I am sure he will be glad to get home again" Lubon nodded to Keeper. "Yes you are right, we always have to bring him back from his (showing off place) but to be fair, Volt still misses his mate, even after all this time, it must be very daunting to be the only Dragon left in the whole of creation" Keeper answered the Yumpoid. "Yes of course you are right Lubon. But nevertheless, Volt is nothing but a big baby, it is time he began to grow up a bit and stop being such a pain, after all he is a Dragon! "

Lubon gestured to the boys to follow him, waved farewell to Keeper, and the three were on their way.

They left Yantron the opposite way from the one they entered. Another set of massive doors began to open slowly on their approach. Archie and Joe waited with Lubon. The first thing they saw, and heard when they stepped to the other side, made the boys gasp. In front of them was the biggest Bee Hive they had ever seen, Farmer Lambert kept bees back home, but never in their lives had the boys seen such enormous Hives,

Archie almost dumbstruck looked at his brother, and said in a quiet voice "How big do you reckon the bees are for these hives?" Joe as worried as his sibling answered. "Well broth, judging by the loud humming around here, they must be massive, I'm not going any further"

Lubon noting the fear in the boys, tried to put them at their ease. "Don't worry Archie and Joe, as I told you earlier, we are all friendly in Yumpland, yes; you will be amazed when you see the bees 'as you call them' but they won't harm you"

With that reassurance, the boys followed the Yumpoid towards the giant beehive. As they came closer, the boys looked around, the noise of humming was almost deafening, and there was something else? It wasn't just a humming, they could hear, there were singing voices as well mingled in.

Just then, Archie had such a surprise, he almost fell over. A giant purple and green creature resembling a bee came from the hive and settled on his shoulder. The boy was transfixed .he stood motionless his eyes darted towards his brother, and in a whisper. "Get it off me our Joe,! Get it off me" Lubon noting the fear, stepped in. "Don't worry Archie, he won't hurt you" The bee like animal, jumped from Archie's shoulder to his hand. The next thing to happen really made the brothers sit up.

"You don't know meeee, but I know youuuu " The bee was actually speaking! Admittedly it sounded very different to the kind of talking Joe and Archie were used to, but it was talking. Archie looked at the coloured bee, he was beautiful. Joe piped up with "That bee is as big as the Magpie's back home, and what's more he can talk!

Just then, a swarm of giant bees, each one a different colour gathered round the boys.
Buzzing and singing. Lubon noting the alarm on the boy's faces, stepped in..
"Now you Baubs, that's quite enough, you are scaring the boys, they are not used to coloured giants like you" With that, the Baubs backed off and sat all over Lubon.
The Yumpoid smiled at the boys. "I suppose these coloured creatures do look a little like bees back in your land. But they are Baubs; and unlike the bees you have back home, these don't have a sting. They do however live in Hives, so there is a similarity but other than that these

are completely different, also the honey, depending on which of the Baubs carried it on his legs ,determines what colour the honey will be"

"So you mean to say your honey is different colours?" Lubon answered the boy. "Well it's like this Archie, depending which flower the pollen comes from, determines what colour the honey will be"   The boy wide eyed, "So you mean, if the flower is red, the honey will be red?" Lubon smiled and nodded his agreement. Archie was intrigued by this, he couldn't imagine honey being any other colour to the
Golden honey he was used to back home.   Just then, without warning the Baubs left Lubon, and gathered round the boys, and in excited voices, they all began to speak at once." Come to the hives and you will seeeee"

Lubon shook his head in amusement. "Now then, you Baubs; don't get so excited. Go ahead, and we will follow" In anticipation as to what they were about to witness next the boys walked, and floated after the Baubs. What they saw almost took their breath away.

Beyond the first Baubhive, amongst trees and flowers there were rows and rows of the
Hives The Baubs clamoured in excited fashion around Lubon, Archie and Joe.
"This one, come and seeeee this one"   The boys followed the chattering creatures through the flowers and trees, mentioning as they went, that they had never seen any of these flowers back home in Granddads Garden.   Nor had they ever heard flowers speak until now!! But there they were, chattering and waving their heads about, some were actually singing, others appeared to be calling the Baubs over to their patch of garden. With shouts of, " Wrong flower, wrong colour, you should know by now, you silly Baubs"

The Baubs, taking little notice of the shouting flowers. Began to split up into groups and make their way to different hives, chattering, and encouraging the boys to follow them. Archie and Joe, not knowing which way to turn, just stood and watched the scene before them.

Each group of Baubs, settled on individual hives, this took a few minutes, when they had all found their homes, everything went suddenly quiet, apart from a low contented humming sound resonating from each hive.

Lubon spoke now. "Come on boys, we will look at the hives, then we must get on our way, don't forget we are looking for Volt" Archie and Joe followed the Yumpoid. With the excitement of the coloured honey and talking flowers they had almost forgotten the lost Dragon. They must find the Dragon and bring him back.

Joe estimated there would be about fifty Baubhives, and as they approached them they were surprised to see each hive was a different colour. How could the Baubs possibly know which hive was which? But they did. Lubon explained to the boys how.
"Well it's like this boys, you see the talking flowers?" Archie and Joe nodded.
Lubon continued. "The Baubs know exactly which bloom to settle on. The Baubs who make pink honey only go to the pink flower's and the ones who make purple honey only go to the purple flower's, Sometimes they make a mistake, but the flower's are pretty good, they put the Baubs right by telling them if they get it wrong and the honey is all colours. Lubon took a deep breath. Mind you, the Baubs get fed up of the bossy flowers telling them what to do but I have to say, the flowers are usually right. We have to reject the honey when that happens" Joe fascinated by this statement asked why.

Lubon trying to suppress a chuckle, "Well Joe, honey made in this way is rather

Potent to say the least" Lubon was recalling the time the Dragon had got hold of some of the 'rainbow 'coloured honey, and they hadn't been able to wake him for a week and when they did finally get the Dragon conscious. He had been acting very silly for days. No, rainbow honey was out of the question. But they would take a pot of purple honey with them, you never know. The boys may be able to tempt Volt into taking a spoonful, especially after hearing the story about the rainbow honey, and the Dragons unfortunate mishap. Lubon suggested that as the boys were only wearing pyjamas, the best way to carry the pot of purple honey would be in a pouch carried on a light harness attached to a strap carried on their back. They could take it in turn to carry the precious cargo.

After saying farewell to the Baubs and the talking flowers, the three set off in search of Volt. Lubon took the lead he was used to the terrain, as they left the Baubs behind. The Yumpoid knew they were on the right trail. He had been this way before. To be honest he wasn't very keen to being here again, strange things happened around this part of YUMPLAND. If you didn't have to be here, then it was best to keep well clear. This place was called RUBBLETON LEDGE. It was so creepy, that some of the YUMP never came within an inch of the area.

Archie and Joe followed Lubon closely. They didn't like the feel of this place. There was a different atmosphere some how. Feeling quite different to the rest of Yumpland Ludon sensing the apprehension in the boy's demeanour, tried to reassure them.

"Don't worry boys I will take care of you, just make sure you stay on the path, and don't move to the left hand side, follow me and whatever you do don't look down try not to be too scared when you hear the loud voices coming from the rocks, we will soon be on the other side"

Archie was the first one to grab his Brothers hand. "Are you frightened our Joe cos I am" the boy's inched slowly after Lubon. They appeared to be entering a dark, damp tunnel. they could hear shouting and moaning coming from the direction they were approaching. They left the tunnel, in front of them the path continued in a straight line. To the right were high cliff's, to the left was what looked like a deep gorge.

Lubon stopped, and said in a quiet voice. "Now Boys do as I tell you, look straight ahead and whatever you do, don't look down"   Lubon began to walk along the narrow path followed by two very nervous boys. All of a sudden there was an ear splitting scream, Joe couldn't help himself, he looked to where the blood curdling noise had come from. Just up above him in the rocks he could make out an ugly big face, with staring red eyes, and as he looked at the monster transfixed, the voice shouted again.

"Mind you don't fall into the deep chasm on the other side of the path: you won't get
out, no, you won't get out. You will be a feast for the giant RUBBLETONS that live down there. They haven't t had a good meal for years. With that the monster roared again. "Go on make a meal of yourselves, we don't want you here, but they will, Oh yes, the RUBBLETONS would love to make a snack of you"   Joe and Archie petrified, just stood quite still.

Lubon, remembering these horrible Rockmonsters, put a comforting arm around each boy. "Don't worry about that bully .Watch this, the Yumpoid taking a handful of something out of his pocket, threw it at the red eyed fiend, with another scream, this time of pain, the monster rock faced horror, crumpled to dust.

Lubon had noticed the boy's distress. "It's alright, Joe and Archie, The Rock monsters are cowards, I should have warned you about them. They can't do anything they just shout a lot. A handful of YAPPER DUST puts them in their place. I always carry some when I come this way. A pinch of that in their faces and they fall apart"

Archie wanted to cry, he was really upset by this latest encounter. Up to now, he and his brother had been frightened by two animals that turned out to be very soft. Archie had love Brak the lion, and the Hippopotamus had been lovely, so had the tortoise, and they had managed to get away from the exploding, ankle grabbing mushroom. Archie shuddered when he thought about those things trying to get his ankles, and he only wearing slippers and pyjamas. Also the colourful Baubs had been really nice.

They were on there way now to find the daft Dragon, Volt had been scary enough, but this was much worse. For the first time since arriving in Yumpland the youngest brother wanted to go home.

Lubon noticing the boy's distress put a comforting arm around his shoulder.
"Come on Archie try not to be so upset, Keeper knows all about the antics of the Rockmonsters, he keeps them under control, unfortunately, although Yumpland is a loving place, where everyone takes care of each other, there are certain elements that try to upset everything. But don't worry, they will never win. For you see Archie, Love always triumphs over evil" Archie wiping away a tear that had escaped from his eyes, sniffed and smiled at the kind Yumpoid.
"Not much further to go now, just a few more steps and we will be away from RUBBLETON LEDGE , we are almost at the Giant mound, I feel sure that is where we will find our missing Dragon"

There was one more dark and brooding tunnel to go through before they reached the giant mound.
Lubon felt a hand within his own, he looked at Archie, "Come on boy, almost there"

The three moved slowly through the slimy dank aperture, from behind them they could hear the Rockmonsters shouting and screaming. Eventually the horrible noises became faint until they could no longer be heard. Soon they were able to see a pinpoint of light.

They walked into lovely bright sunshine, and almost immediately they were confronted by Volt.

"You took your time; I thought you would never come?" Archie and Joe were delighted to see the Dragon. Volt cleared his throat, and as he did, a flame of fire, shot over the top of Lubon's heads. The Dragon spluttered and coughed
"Sorry about that, Before we go any further, I have been in deep thought, concerning the honey incident, and I have to tell you, that I believe I was too hasty, you were only trying to help, and to be quite honest with you, this fire business is driving me nuts, so I will try the honey method before my throat gets sore beyond help, and in a pleading voice. "I don't suppose you have any with you?"

Joe and Archie looked at each other and smiled. Joe felt in his pouch
 and pulled out the pot of purple honey. The Dragon, Pleased to see the pot of balm, gave a sudden roar, as he did a pall of smoke and fire shot from his mouth. Volt cried out
"Oh my poor throat, I am fed up now, really fed up, please help me"

Lubon and the boys looked up at the Dragon. How were they going to get the honey intro that huge Mouth?
This would take some working out. Volt was enormous, as big as the cottage back home. The boys had thought this out when they first met him. Joe had an idea.
"How about putting the honey on one of Volt's big feet, then he could lick it off"

Further Secrets of the Garden

The Dragon piped up, "Mm, don't fancy that, you don't know where my feet have been"

Then Archie came up with the perfect solution. He called out to the Dragon.
"How about you lying down on your tummy, putting your head on your big paws
and we will tip the honey into your mouth"

Lubon nodded his approval. He called up to the Dragon, "What do you think to that idea Volt" The reply came.

"Excellent Lubon, excellent, move well back all of you and I will lower myself down as far as I can"
So with the shake of his wings, causing a tirade of dust and loose scales, Volt lowered his mighty bulk down to the floor. Lubon and the boys waited for the Dragon to settle his giant head on his feet.

Volt looked into the faces of the three little helpers, and they looked at him. Volt opened his mouth to speak. "This is so kind of you; especially as I went off in a huff,
I am such a silly old Dragon at times" With that, another plume of fire left his mouth, just missing Lubon's hat.
"Oh dear, there I go again, please help me to stop this, my teeth are getting burned to a crisp as well as my throat being sore, and I stink of smoke, horrible"

Lubon addressed Joe who was carrying the pouch of honey. "Can you suggest how best to administer the honey; or you Archie, how do you think we should do it?"
As the boys pondered, the question, The Dragon provided the answer. With a mighty
Roar Volt opened his enormous jaws. The boys were looking into the cavernous mouth of the Dragon.
Lubon gestured to Joe, "Quick boy, the honey. Joe without further ado took the pouch from its strap and gave it to the Yumpoid. The three ventured forward, towards the gaping chasm that was Volt's mouth.

Lubon spoke with a worried sounding voice. "It needs to reach the throat, in order to do the most good; the honey must touch his throat"

Archie, without showing the slightest fear said. "I'm the smallest; I'll do it, and with no further thought the young boy climbed up onto the Dragons jaw. Joe, with concern in his voice spoke to his brother, "Be careful Arch, Volt could close his mouth anytime, and you would be trapped" Joe shuddered at the thought. Lubon spoke to the Dragon, as calmly as he could.
"Now Volt, try to help Archie, don't take any deep breaths, keep your mouth open as wide as you can, and whatever you do. Don't talk the boy is trying to help you"

By this time the Dragon was cross eyed. For one thing, his jaw was tickling where the boy was wriggling about with his attempt to get inside the mouth, and another, his tongue was becoming dry, and his eyes were watering. He would have to cough in a moment, he would just have to.
As Archie got a foot hold, and managed to scramble onto the Dragon's tongue, Volt could hold back no more, with a mighty explosion he puffed out a pall of smoke. Quick as a flash Archie managed to wriggle under the Dragons tongue. The flames that followed the smoke missed him, apart from a tiny scorch mark where the flame caught his hair, as it shot out in the direction of Lubon and Joe. The Yumpoid and Joe just managed to duck as the fire streaked above them. The elder brother began to scream in terror.
"Archie, don't be dead, please don't be dead" The Dragon had half closed his mouth.
He was mortified that he hadn't been able to control the flame throwing. He felt wretched. Was the boy injured? Volt began to cry proper Dragon tears. Suddenly, he felt a tickle under his tongue. Could the boy be alright? Volt opened his mouth as wide as he was able.

From beneath the Dragons tongue, came an arm holding the pot of purple honey. Then the boy emerged. "It's ok Broth I'm fine. He waved the honey towards Lubon and Joe. "I'm just going to crawl to the back of Volts tongue, and pour this all over his throat. See if it will stop him flame throwing"

Archie, with the honey back in the strap for safety, began to crawl towards the back of the Dragons enormous mouth. it felt very strange, sort of warm, with a smell of spent firework's when they've gone out, and the teeth, my goodness they were big, Archie estimated the back ones especially must be as big as table legs, some very yellow, one or two needed fillings, but Archie didn't reckon the Dragon ever saw a dentist' Archie mused to himself the Dragon was lucky. He personally didn't like going to the dentist at all.

If a Dragon can show emotion, well Volt did just that. His tears of sorrow turned to those of joy, in fact he actually chuckled, but that was because. Archie was tickling. his tongue. Volt heaved a big sigh of relief as he felt the soothing honey trickle down the back of his throat. The boys had been right. Honey did soothe the throat. He must reward them for their kindness; he would take them to his cave on their return, and make a gift of something he was sure the boys would like.

Archie was worried about turning round in the Dragon's mouth, so after administering the soothing balm, he began very carefully to crawl backwards. Eventually he arrived at the front of the mouth, just under Volts nose. Archie lifted his head, and was looking into the left nostril. It was huge, and very dark. It reminded the boy of the time they had visited the caves when they went to Somerset for a holiday one year.
That had been awesome' but not as awesome as this.

He came out of the Dragon's mouth feet first. Joe and Lubon who had been watching and waiting with baited breath gave a cheer. The elder brother secretly thought his sibling very brave. Archie scrambled down to the ground to be greeted with a hug from Joe and a pat on the back from the Yumpoid.

Archie felt quite special, it wasn't every day he got praise from Joe, and it wasn't every day he crawled inside the mouth of an enormous Dragon.

When the three little helpers had finished hugging and patting backs Volt looked down at them and spoke.
"Now Boy's and Lubon, can I just say this, you have done a wonderful thing, and smiling, said "See, 'I am speaking, and not spitting out fire," With that the Dragon
Pursed his lips and attempted to blow. But not even a puff of smoke could be seen.

A cloud suddenly appeared on his face. "But aren't Dragons supposed to breathe fire, and scare people?" Lubon chipped in. "Don't worry Volt , it doesn't mean you will never have fire in your belly, after all as you pointed out, Dragon's are supposed breathe fire, but not every time they open their mouths as you have been doing causing you such a sore throat"

Volt smiled at the Yumpoid and said "That's ok then, after all I do need to be a bit horrible. Especially when I fly over RUBBLETON LEDGE and those nasty ROCK MONSTERS I do have my reputation to consider you know."
Lubon shook his head at the contrary Dragon, smiled, and said nothing.

The Dragon, sounding very important, spoke to Lubon, and the boys. "Now if you will excuse me for a moment while I say farewell to my mate, then we will be on our way" With that Volt headed to the mound. He arrived back a few moments later, with what looked like a tear in his eye. He looked at the three. "Please forgive me, but it doesn't get any easier, knowing I am the only Dragon left. My mate was difficult to live with and got me down at times, but I still miss her"

The Dragon cheered up now. He was about to do a kindness in return, and that   always made him feel better. "Would you like a ride back to my cave" Archie and Joe nodded, they would love a ride. It had been a long walk, especially in slippers.

Volt in a grown up voice said "Climb on my back, you first Archie, then Joe, and finally Lubon. If you hang onto my neck Archie, hang on tight mind, and Joe and Lubon sit behind my wings, we will be well balanced."

When the passengers were safely on board. and everything was ready for take off Volt flapped his giant wings . Once again bits of dead skin, and scales flew off in every direction. Making the passengers cough and sneeze. With a giant whoosh of his wings the Dragon was airborne.

Up and up they went, towards the blue cloudless sky, they flew over the Dark tunnel. Volt seemed to pick up speed; the three passengers let out a yell as the Dragon banked towards RUBBLETON LEDGE. With giant wings outstretched, Volt hurtled towards the ROCKMOMSTER, he opened his mouth and with a mighty puff he let the red eyed fiend know just what he thought of him, as the flame reached the rock there was a mighty screech from the cowardly black mountain. Volt let out a yell of triumph. Nobody messed with the Dragon.

They flew over the Upside Down Forrest; they flew over YANTRON just as the Laser lights were starting the giant clock like mechanism. Volt shouted to his passengers to cover their ears and eyes for a moment. As showers of light shot in every direction. And thunderous music began to play.

Next came the pond with the noisy blue fish. As they glided over the frothing watery
Hullabaloo, Archie who had the best view, suddenly saw what he believed could be the answer to the question of the more timid pink and white fish being scared all the time. He called out to Joe and Lubon.

"Can you see what I see?" The two, From their position, looked down towards the foaming pond. Archie continued " Do you see another, smaller pond alongside the other?"
Joe answered his Brother. " Yes, but what about it?"
Archie, in excited fashion, "There seems to be a channel between the two. Why don't we try to clear a way for the quieter fish to escape to the smaller pond when we get back down to YUMPLAND?"
Lubon was then first to answer. " That sounds like a very good idea Archie, of course, this is the first time I have seen the pond, or anything else for that matter from this position, but that is an excellent idea, let us get back then we can arrange something"

Volt, who had been listening to the banter between his passengers, also thought the idea a good one; another person who would be happy was SPIK. The big bird was also was fed up with the noisy blue fish.

Eventually after what seemed an age, Volt began the descent to where he had begun the journey when he was a very disgruntled Dragon, all because he hadn't understood the Boy Archie, when he had offered honey for his sore throat. Now he understood though, Yes the purple honey had done the trick and his sore throat was under control. He would make a point of asking the Baub's if they would be so kind as to supply him with plenty of the soothing potion. After all, Volt quite liked the colourful creatures, and he quite liked the sweet taste of purple honey as it trickled down his throat.

YUMPLAND was coming closer and closer. "Hang on tight," shouted the Dragon.
But he had rather miss timed his landing. With a thud Volt landed hard. Joe and Lubon slid down the scaly wings bang, onto the ground. Joe gave a loud yell "Oh my bum" Archie who had hung on tight to the Dragon's neck was still high in the air.

Volt gave Archie a cheeky wink, "Glad you enjoyed your treat boy" and as he did, he bent his long neck towards the other two travellers, and placed Archie, ever so gently onto the floor at their feet.

Joe stood up rubbing his bottom. He looked up to see the Dragon smiling down at him showing his brown and green teeth.
"That wasn't funny Dragon" Volt continued to smile. And answered the disgruntled boy.
" Well it was- from where I'm standing"
With that Volt walked towards his cave, still laughing.

Lubon had landed unscathed. He turned to Joe and said. "Don't take any notice of the Dragon, it's just one of his silly games, He's always up to one trick or another" Then, addressing both boys Lubon said.
 "Now come on we have much to do before you go back to your own Land, first I suggest we have something to eat and drink, then we can tackle the job of making a new home for the timid fish"

CHAPTER 16

GOING HOME

Lubon reckoned the idea a good one, he had thought long and hard how best to help the timid fish; he had felt sorry for them for quite a long time. But until now a solution hadn't been forthcoming. But now since the view from above, the answer was pretty obvious. He would talk to the other Yumpoid's- and tell them of his adventure and what he had seen from the air. But first he would have a word with Keeper. That was the correct thing to do. He must also talk to him about the boy's returning home, because he realised that the allotted time for their visit was almost over. The time spent on YUMPLAND was now almost the equivalent of one night back in their land and it would soon be morning there. Besides Archie and Joe Potts belonged at home with their own people and their own Gnomes.

The YUMPOID found Keeper where the leader spent a lot of his time, at the seeing pool.
After a talk, it was decided, that as a last adventure, the boy's, along with some of the YUMPOIDS could construct a narrow trench between the two ponds to enable the timid fish to escape the noisy blue ones.

"That was an excellent idea of the young boy's Lubon, so it is only fitting that he and his brother should help build a safe retreat for the pink and white fish. Will you tell them of my decision, but inform them that there isn't much time left, it must be done at once" Lubon thanked Keeper, and left to inform the boys what had been said.

So with buckets, shovels and lots of determination, work to make a channel began amidst a lot of chattering, complaining and shouting from the blue fish.

First it was decided, that the best way to do the job was to dig a shallow ditch between the two ponds allowing just enough room for the timid fish. Then an opening would be made in each pond. And the pink and white fish could swim to safety to a pond of their own. So with Archie and YUMPOIDS, digging one end, and Joe and Lubon at the other, a channel was soon constructed. Then it was time to dig a gap in the sides of each pond and let the water, and the timid fish find their way to the other safer side.

Lubon addressed the timid fish. "Now it is time for you to begin a much happier life.
The boy' Archie came up with a splendid solution to your problem, you are to move to a new home away from the blue fish, now do exactly as you are told, and everything will flow smoothly"

On hearing this, the blue fish began to thrash about angrily in the water causing it to foam and bubble.
"Why should they be given a new home, the little babies, what about us?" Just then from nowhere, SPIK the colourful bird, with his bright yellow breast landed by the side of the frothing pond.

He opened his enormous white beak. "QUIET YOU NOISY FISH, It serves you right for being so horrible to the little pink and blue fish, they are moving to a new and better place away from you"
All of a sudden the pond was calm. The Blue fish had seen the yellow colour on the big bird, and as we know, Yellow puts the fish to sleep.

Lubon clapped his hands loudly, he didn't care much for the noisy blue fish, but he realised that if they went to sleep they could drown. After a while they awoke, but they were less noisy now, they didn't like yellow at all, so it was in their interest to keep quiet.

Eventually the channel was dug just deep enough for the timid fish to swim to their new pond. As the little fish swam to a happier life, they sang a sweet little song.

" Thank you Archie, Thank you Joe, you've made us happy, as to our new home we go"

The boys, and the YUMPOIDS, had done a wonderful job. Keeper was happy Volt was happy, in fact everyone in YUMPLAND was happy for the little fish.

Lubon spoke now. "Well Archie and Joe, it is almost time for you to be making your way home to your planet. But first, we have another surprise for you. Keeper has something to tell you"

Archie and Joe, intrigued as to what was going to happen next, waited for the big man with his magic staff to arrive. Meanwhile they decided to have a walk around YUMPLAND for the last time. As the boys visited places they had been whilst on this wonderful planet, they were accompanied by first LUMA the Hippopotamus. Then BRAK the lion, they visited the Upside down Forrest. The exploding Mushrooms were quieter now, not so much snapping and biting at your ankles. Archie hadn't liked the mushroom's much. To tell the truth they had scared him, and the red colour was horrible. It got in his slippers and up his nose. As they walked along SPIK the big bird came to join them. As usual he was preening and showing off. He flapped his beautiful wings. And in his usual haughty fashion he said to the boy's

"I bet you are glad you met lovely me?" Archie and Joe looked at each other. True SPIK was lovely, his colours were beautiful, like a rainbow they sometimes had at home, but to be honest, like they had already realised, he was too big headed.

BRAK the lion, who was walking along side the boys, turned to Archie, and said.

"Try not to take too much notice of the pompous show off, we don't, we find it better to let him get on with it. After all he does have his good side, the blue fish for instant. If it wasn't for SPIK keeping them under control, they would drive us all mad with their constant shouting and arguing." With that the lion, rubbed his head on the boy's shoulder. Archie put out his hand and stroked the thick mane at the same time nuzzling. Closely to BRAK, thinking to himself, just how wonderful and magical this really was.

And once again surmising that nobody would ever believe this.

The boys visited the BAUBS, who on seeing the boys again tried to sit all over them like they had Lubon earlier. Archie reminding them not to forget to give VOLT a regular supply of purple honey, They also looked in on the talking flowers, their chatter had really made the boys laugh. They had thought it fascinating how the flowers directed the BAUBS onto the correct bloom in order they would have the right colour honey. This whole business was almost unbelievable to both boys. But it was nevertheless true.

Archie and Joe made their way to the Dragons cave, he had promised them something special. And they wanted to find out what it was. They had just reached the entrance to the dark chamber, when they heard the Dragon's voice.

"I thought you were never going to get here, come on boys we haven't much time now. Keeper has been looking for you." Archie and Joe hurried as fast as they could into the cave.   Volt looking very important ushered the boys to the back of the cave.

"Now then Archie and Joe, I would like you to witness this before you go back to your own land. Do you remember being told about how special this place really is?"

Both boy's nodded; this seemed to be very important to the Dragon.
"Do you see that extra bright light on the wall?" Once again the boys nodded.
"He has just arrived, he is a special Yumpoid, much loved by all here in YUMPLAND. Very soon he will have many visitors; every one loves this place.
Archie piped up." What do you mean special what happened to him?"

The Dragon smiled at the boy, " Don't you remember what you were told" Archie shook his head. " Well its like this, all Yumpoid's end their days here, its special place, they just live on shining their special light forever."   Joe asked in a hushed tone.
"Does it mean they are all dead?"

Volt seeing the fear in the boys eyes, assured him that that, wasn't the case.
"Nobody dies here boy, the older Yumpoid's when they grow tired, rest here, there is no such thing as death, they just shine on the wall forever, rested and happy each in his own colour, and visited on a regular basis by the other Yumpoid's."

Archie and Joe gazed around the huge cave; it really was a very special place. Millions of lights shone and twinkled; it did seem a very happy place. Volt was right.

The Dragon addressed the boys once more. "Now about the other business. Didn't you say you would like a treasure to take home" Both boy's nodded.
"Well take a look round my cave, there must be a little something that takes your fancy"

Archie remembered the Dragon's baby teeth, nice and white, scattered on the floor of the cave. " Can I have a baby tooth please?" Volt let out a huge laugh. "My baby teeth, and shaking his large head from side to side, why would you want those?"

The boy answered the amused Dragon" Cos one would fit very nicely in my pyjama pocket. Volt scratched his head, causing more flakes of skin to cascade all over the Cave floor, and the boys. " Funny boy" and turning his attention to Joe, " I suppose you want something just as daft?"

Joe brushing himself down, coughed loudly, as bits of dead skin got into his mouth. He had seen something that looked like a piece of flint Granddad had shown him once. "Can I have that?" He said to the Dragon, pointing to article of his choice on the floor, just inside the cave.

Archie asked his brother why he would want an old piece of flat coal. Joe answered.
"Don't you remember Arch, we lost the drawbridge to our LEGGO SET Fort. I just thought it would make a good replacement if we ask Dad to make a bracket to attach it to the wall of the fort, what do you think?" Archie was impressed by his brother's idea He hadn't thought of it.

Volt listening to the boys chatter, thought they must have some funny ideas back in their land, but if that was what they wanted' who was he to say the couldn't.

So with a piece of flint and a baby tooth the brothers left the Dragons cave, after first saying goodbye to all the YUMPLIGHTS, scattered around the vast cave walls.

Archie and Joe didn't want to say goodbye to The Dragon, he was funny and lovely and they would miss him.

Volt was going to miss the boy's, they had done such a wonderful thing for him, and his throat would be fine now. He had made pact with the BAUBS to supply him with purple honey for his throat. In turn it had been decided to take them for a ride on his Back now and again, after all

Dragons can fly much higher than BAUBS. Volt had chuckled at the idea, he would give them the ride of their lives, and he knew a few moves that would make their tummies do a summersault.

Lubon arrived on the scene. "Come on boys, Keeper is waiting for you, its almost time for you to leave YUMPLAND, and do try to smarten yourselves up a bit before you meet our leader again. You are both covered in dirt of one sort and another" Archie and Joe looked up at the Dragon. Volt was displaying a sad face; all of a sudden he stooped down until he had eye contact with both boys.

"Don't worry too much about the YUMPOID dirt it will soon disappear before you go home. I will never forget you, but never fear I will be keeping watch on you both. Sometimes you will think you see me. Other times you will feel my presence, I love you Archie and Joe"
Volt blinked, and as he did two enormous tears trickled down his horny scaly face.
The boys overcome with emotion began to cry. "We will miss you too Volt"

The Dragon not wanting the boys to be upset blew his nose loudly and said "Why the tears?" Aren't we silly we will always be friends, I will be here, and you will be there. Every time we think of each other. We will be close, and as I told you, I will never be far away and another thing you may like to know, in a hundred years time at the next Awakening of your Gnomes- you won't be here, but I will, so I can tell your grandchildren all about how kind you have been to me, whilst you have been in YUMPLAND"

The boys left the cave, followed by the Dragon, and went with Lubon to meet Keeper. They hadn't gone very far when they were joined by a multitude of shouting, cheering YUMPOID Residents.

"This way Archie and Joe; this way" The boys were escorted to YANTRON. Once inside the giant place, they were confronted to the biggest party they had ever been to in their lives, Music played; BEEMINS floated about holding gold trays full of delicious food. Archie and Joe remembered these coloured orbs from their own garden party when Granddad was alive. They tucked into their favourite meal, and enjoyed spending time with all new friends.

LUMA the Hippopotamus, and BRAK the lion, kept close to the boys, TRUG. The Two headed Tortoise enjoyed eating with both mouths at the same time. Nobody seemed to think that odd. Volt secretly thought the tortoise rather greedy, but he didn't say anything. A sweet smell of honey brew seemed to be wafting around YANTRON, everybody was happy.

It was almost time for the boys to leave this enchanting place. Archie and Joe feeling very tired now looked around this magic place, they would never forget YUMPLAND, and all these wonderful people and animals, and they would especially always remember Volt the wonderful Dragon.

Keeper entered the giant YANTRON. He stood in the centre of the Hall.
"Now Archie and Joe Potts, it really is time to go. We love you, and we will never forget your kindness. And for a special present, I am going to allow just enough magic to accompany you down the Gnome beam so you may have a last magic party for all our honorary brother Gnomes back in your own garden. Also we would like you to accept this tiny casket to be opened on your return home. Archie looked up to Keeper and asked what it was. Keeper smiled at the boy." It is a gift of talking seeds, plant then in a sunny position. Water them with kindness, keep it to yourselves, and who knows perhaps on a warm summer day they may have a word or two with you both, of course you understand that they will only speak when you are

alone with them, and it must remain secret, After all your Land isn't ready for flowers you can have a conversation with?" Archie took the tiny box in his hand. And whispered "Thank you Keeper"

 The great man continued" But I am afraid that will be it as far as parties go for another hundred years. I know we exceeded the rule this time, because of your love and caring about our planet and your Gnomes, but we can't do it too often. The rule states that your Gnomes come to life every hundred years. As long as the love continues, down the Potts line. So from now on that rule must be adhered to.

Archie and Joe thanked Keeper for allowing them the adventure of travelling up the Gnome beam to YUMPLAND and meeting all the wonderful creatures that lived there.

All of a sudden, from out side YANTRON there was a whooshing sound. Keeper called the boys. "Come on its time to go, the Gnome beam won't wait"
In an instant the boys were aboard. The familiar warm glow seemed to surround the boys, and in an instant, the pyjamas and slippers that had been decidedly dirty were instantly clean, as they had been before arriving in this magical place. The Gnome beam seemed to travelling at a terrific speed, they past galaxies, stars, unknown planets.

Archie and Joe felt their tummies doing cartwheels, like they remembered experiencing each time they went boring shopping with their Mum as they sometimes went in the lift in the arcade. Joe reckoned it was a pretty similar feeling, but much more tummy turning.
 But as quick as you like they were back in their beds still fast asleep. And it was almost morning.

CHAPTER 17

HOME

Archie was the first to awake; he had had a funny dream. He lay trying to gather his thoughts. There had been a Dragon, a funny Dragon, and lots of strange creatures. Some nice, some, not so nice. Just then there was a call from downstairs.

It was Sylvia their mother. "Come on boys it's almost time to get up. Your breakfast will soon be on the table" Joe awoke with a start." Is that you Volt"
Archie on hearing his brother's word's leaped out of bed.
"What did you just say our Joe?" Joe bleary eyed and half asleep sat up and rubbing his eyes, he answered "Volt, I said Volt' Archie excited now, "So it wasn't a dream then; They had shared an adventure? .   They had been to YUMPLAND? It was real.
Wasn't it exciting? They had seen a real Dragon. They had met Keeper and all the other wonderful creatures.
Archie felt in his pyjama pocket, yes, there was the Baby tooth from the floor of the Dragon's cave, and there was the tiny casket. He gestured to his brother. "Where do you reckon we ought to put this stuff?" Joe answered after first feeling in his own pocket, yes there was the piece of flat coal like block of hard substance.
"What about Granddads box in the workshop, nobody but us knows anything about that?" Archie nodded his agreement to the suggestion.

From downstairs there was another call " Do you want cold porridge, now get up at once the pair of you?" "Dad wants you to help him shovel the snow away from the path"

The boys not wanting to raise suspicion washed and hurried down to the warm kitchen

And tucked into their breakfast. Jenny spoke; "Would you both like a spoon honey on your porridge as usual" Their Granny pulled the pot of honey towards her. The boys looked at each other and gave a secretive grin. They both nodded. Jenny, noting the humour, shook her head and smiled. What on earth was tickling her Grandchildren now?"

"Well boys; its Christmas Eve, are you ready for the big day?" Archie a mouthful of sweet porridge nodded to Jenny. She continued.
"As soon as you can your Dad is waiting for you outside, he want to get the paths clear.
There was another heavy fall of snow last night, and judging by what was going on in the early hours, lights flashing funny noises, the council lorries must have been at it half the night, trying to keep the roads clear for the traffic that's expected on them today"

Of course what Jenny and her Son and Daughter-in -law had heard in the night, wasn't only support vehicles clearing snow packed roads, it was the Gnome beam coming to collect the boys for the adventure and their return in the magic beam this morning. The meal was delicious, both boys eating as fast as they dare, without being told off by their mum for gulping the food.

Suddenly there was a scraping sound outside the door and Fred Potts came into the kitchen. He was dressed in heavy clothes, and boots. Rubbing his hands together over the blazing fire, he said. In a shivery voice…
"Come on boys, I thought you were never going to get up today, there is much to do. All the paths around the cottage are piled high with driven snow, you can't even get down to the workshop"

That statement brought the boys back to Earth with a bang, they must get to MOLAC

And the other Gnomes, and tell them all about the adventure.

Archie spoke with eagerness, "Can me and Joe clear the path to the Workshop Dad"
Fred' pleased with this helpful attitude smiled at his youngest son.

"Yes Son as soon as you like. You will find a couple of shovels by the back door,
But get your warm clothes on first, its bitter out there"

Both boys booted and dressed for the arctic by their fussy mother stepped out into the winter weather.

They trudged gingerly around the side of the cottage. Fred had made a good start.
But there was much to do before they could make their way to the workshop.

After what seemed like ages, they were beginning to make headway. Eventually
The boys could see the workshop door. Another few steps and they were within reach of the goal.

Then from the kitchen, they heard their mother " Lunch is ready boys," Archie not wanting to be bothered with dinner, let out a loud yell. "Can we have another few minutes Mum; we are nearly there"

Sylvia in her usual manner, "Now boys please, I don't think for one moment you would enjoy cold casserole"

Joe, teeth chattering; nose red.   "Come on Broth we can come back later. Besides I feel hungry now, and Mums casserole is pretty yummy"

Archie, also feeling cold agreed with Joe that a rest and a warming meal would go down a treat.

By the time they got back to the job in hand it was almost dark. They managed to pull the door of the workshop open. There they were, all the Gnomes, just as they had left them, and it was decided that as soon as possible the two broken chaps would be mended. First ABLEG would be put right, then the lesser gnome would be mended.

Unfortunately there wasn't going to be time to tell MOLAC and the others about the adventure, Their mother had been adamant. But they would however, have just enough time to put the secret presents from Keeper into the box hidden behind the shelf.

Their mother called again this time in her (I am getting angry) voice

"One more hour, then in for a bath and early to bed. We have a lot to do tonight; mince pies to make, and stuffing for the turkey. After all, you don't want to miss your Christmas dinner do you" Besides, if you aren't asleep when Santa comes you won't get any presents"

The boys knew it was no use arguing, So reluctantly they made their way to the cottage.

Somehow Christmas didn't seem as exciting as it usually did. But how could it after the awesome adventure they had just enjoyed.

They needn't have worried though, for the magic was about to continue for a while yet.

After a bath, and hair washed, with the usual screeching and yelling from Archie as the soap went in his eyes, and similarly when his nails were cut. The boys were given time to hang their pillow cases at the foot of each bed, then they were tucked up with a hot milk drink, and a goodnight kiss.

The boys awoke on a cold crisp Christmas morning to the smell of fried bacon and egg.

Archie was the first out of bed. He tried to show interest in his bulging cotton case, but somehow he felt rather sad. Joe was next to surface from under his warm Duvet.

The boys investigated their presents. Archie quite liked the football and new boots, the
Tent he had asked Santa for was excellent, he also thought the new DVD'S were good.
Just then something right in the corner of the pillowcase took his attention. The excited boy shouted to his brother."
Joe quick, look what I've found in my presents.

Joe intrigued hurried to his brother. Archie opened his fingers, There in the palm of his hand were two of the Dragons scales.
The brothers looked at each other, how did Volts scales get into the pillowcase?"
Joe rushed back to his own half- empty sack. He pulled out the remaining presents as quick as he could. And would you believe it. There- nestling in one corner, was a tiny pot of purple honey.

The boy's were overawed. This was wonderful; Archie turned to his brother.
"What does it mean our Joe?" The elder brother shook his head. "Don't know Arch, but I'll tell you something I do know, Christmas has taken on a much better feeling, something smashing has just happened" Archie- full of excitement. Began to jump up and down, "Does it mean that Volt has been to our house since we came home?"
Joe didn't know the answer to that question, and what's more there was nobody to ask.

The Brothers- light of spirit now, went downstairs to begin their Christmas celebrations, and later on today they must make some excuse to go to the workshop and put these latest magic trophies in Granddads box with the other bits of treasure. Also they must tell MOLAC and the other Gnomes about the extra planned Gnome beam party for later in the year. But how would they tell them. How much of the new magic would they understand?"

The boys managed to get away for a while after lunch, when their Mum and Dad were having a nap. As they were leaving to go to the workshop Jenny, their Granny followed them,

"Care to tell me what's been going on, you may be able to fool your Mum and Dad but not me. You two are up to something. Is it something to do with the magic and the Gnomes?" The boys stopped and turning round to their Gran. Should they tell her about YUMPLAND and the Dragon called Volt, and if they did, would she understand?" Archie and Joe looked at each other and knew exactly what they were going to do.

"Come on Gran, you knew about the Gnome Beam party when Granddad was alive,
So we feel sure you will continue to keep the secret about our latest adventure, Archie looked at Jenny
"But Gran this is far more amazing, than anything before. If we tell you, will you promise to keep the secret? Jenny took her Grandsons hand and went with then to Billy's Workshop. Of course she knew the stories of Gnome Beam night were all true, she hadn't believed at first, after all it was pretty magic stuff. But she had experienced Billy's favourite Gnome MOLAC coming to life, so yes she did believe the magic.

Archie and Joe, were a couple of dreamers just like her Billy. Of course she would keep the lovely SECRET OF THE GARDEN. It had all been part of her Billy.
The three went towards the Workshop Jenny wasn't sure what would happen from now on, but one thing she did know, and that was she wanted more than anything to be part of the ongoing adventure of MOLAC, and the rest of this magical story.

THE END   (Or is it")